ZADIG
AND OTHER STORIES

DOVER THRIFT EDITIONS

Voltaire

DOVER PUBLICATIONS, INC.
MINEOLA, NEW YORK

DOVER THRIFT EDITIONS

GENERAL EDITOR: SUSAN L. RATTINER
EDITOR OF THIS VOLUME: STEPHANIE CASTILLO SAMOY

Bibliographical Note

Zadig and Other Stories, first published by Dover Publications, Inc., in 2020, is a new compilation of works by Voltaire, reprinted from authoritative sources. A new introductory note has been specially prepared for this volume.

International Standard Book Number

ISBN-13: 978-0-486-84250-9
ISBN-10: 0-486-84250-9

Manufactured in the United States by LSC Communications
84250901
www.doverpublications.com
2 4 6 8 10 9 7 5 3 1
2020

Note

I always made one prayer to God, a very short one.
Here it is: "O Lord, make our enemies quite ridiculous!"
God granted it.
> —Voltaire's Letter to Étienne Noël Damilaville
> 16 May 1767

ALTHOUGH FRANÇOIS-MARIE AROUET (1694–1778) wrote enough in his long life to fill a substantial library, he never definitively explained the meaning or origin of his famous pen name Voltaire. A great believer in freedom, this oversight on his part leaves us, however, free to speculate that, foreseeing his long career to come as a wit, satirist, philosopher, historian, poet, and dramatist, a good part of which would be spent attacking, or at least annoying, his philosophical opponents and his critics, the pen name might protect him somewhat from retribution. If, indeed, that was the idea, Voltaire was wrong. His unquenchable enmity to organized religion, fanaticism, intolerance, ignorance, and superstition provoked the authorities, political, philosophical, and religious, sufficiently for any one life, but he replied to the criticism and attacks primarily with his wits, sometimes also with the establishment of some geographical distance from those who could do him harm. At the vantage point of over two-and-a-half centuries, it looks like a wise and winning strategy. The names of his adversaries are known today mostly to scholars, but the world still reads Voltaire.

Among the many sharp tools in Voltaire's arsenal for attacking and annoying whatever he felt deserved attacking and annoying was the philosophical tale, and the greatest of Voltaire's tales was *Candide*. The reader who enjoyed *Candide* will find in this volume six more examples of Voltaire's short fiction, the substantial novella *Zadig*, first published in 1747, and five other shorter tales. It isn't necessary here to recount the improbably convoluted plot of *Zadig*—let the surprises come where they come while the reader enjoys the trials and tribulations of the young philosopher from ancient Babylon who only wants to accomplish good things and to be happy, and finds himself thwarted and confounded at every turn. One of the great rewards of Voltaire's fiction is that almost everything can be, and indeed has been, found there—the Enlightenment's outlook on organized religion and primitive superstition, but also much more than that. Critics and historians of fictional genres have found the origins of modern science fiction in Voltaire's speculations about intergalactic space travel in the story *Micromégas*, also reprinted here, and devotees of the modern mystery story have found in Zadig's earnestly rational approach to the world some of the vague beginnings of the modern detective story. With Voltaire, you will always find more than you're looking for. It only depends on how deeply you enjoy the journey.

—John Grafton
Princeton, New Jersey
May 2020

Contents

ZADIG, OR DESTINY

AN EASTERN TALE

CERTIFICATE OF APPROVAL.—I, the undersigned, who have succeeded in making myself pass for a man of learning and even of wit, have read this manuscript, and found it, in spite of myself, curious and amusing, moral and philosophical, and worthy even of pleasing those who hate romances. So I have disparaged it, and assured the cadi that it is an abominable work.

DEDICATORY EPISTLE OF ZADIG TO
THE SULTANA SHERAH, BY SADI.

The 10th day of the month Shawal, in the year 837 of the Hegira.

Delight of the eyes, torment of the heart, and lamp of the soul, I kiss not the dust of thy feet, because thou dost scarcely ever walk, or only on Persian carpets or over rose leaves. I present thee with the translation of a book written by an ancient sage, to whom, being in the happy condition of having nothing to do, there occurred the happy thought of amusing himself by writing the story of Zadig, a work that means more than it seems to do. I beseech thee to read it and form thy judgment on it; for although thou art in the springtime of life, and courted by pleasures of every kind; although thou art fair, and thy talents add to thy beauty; and although thou art loaded with praises from morning to night, and so hast every right to be devoid of common sense, yet thou hast a very sound intelligence and a highly refined taste, and I have heard thee argue better than any old dervish with a long beard and pointed cap. Thou art cautious yet not suspicious; thou art gentle without being weak; thou art beneficent with due discrimination; thou dost love thy friends, and makest to

1

thyself no enemies. Thy wit never borrows its charm from the shafts of slander; thou dost neither say nor do evil, in spite of abundant facilities if thou wert so inclined. Lastly, thy soul has always appeared to me as spotless as thy beauty. Thou hast even a small stock of philosophy, which has led me to believe that thou wouldst take more interest than any other of thy sex in this work of a wise man.

It was originally written in ancient Chaldean, which neither thou nor I understand. It was translated into Arabic for the entertainment of the famous Sultan Oulook, about the time when the Arabs and Persians were beginning to compose *The Thousand and One Nights*, *The Thousand and One Days*, etc. Oulook preferred to read *Zadig*; but the ladies of his harem liked the others better.

"How can you prefer," said the wise Oulook, "senseless stories that mean nothing?"

"That is just why we are so fond of them," answered the ladies.

I feel confident that thou wilt not resemble them, but that thou wilt be a true Oulook; and I venture to hope that when thou art weary of general conversation, which is of much the same character as *The Arabian Nights Entertainment*, except that it is less amusing, I may have the honor of talking to thee for a few minutes in a rational manner. If thou hadst been Thalestris in the time of Alexander, son of Philip, or if thou hadst been the Queen of Sheba in the days of Solomon, those kings would have traveled to thee, not thou to them.

I pray the heavenly powers that thy pleasures may be unalloyed, thy beauty unfading, and thy happiness everlasting.

Chapter 1

The Man of One Eye

IN THE TIME of King Moabdar there lived at Babylon a young man named Zadig, who was born with a good disposition, which education had strengthened. Though young and rich, he knew how to restrain his passions; he was free from all affectation, made no pretension to infallibility himself, and knew how to respect the foibles of others. People were astonished to see that, with all his wit, he never turned his powers of raillery on the vague, disconnected, and confused talk, the rash censures, the ignorant judgments, the scurvy jests, and all that vain babble of words which went by the name of conversation at Babylon. He had learned in the first book of Zoroaster that self-conceit is a bladder puffed up with wind, out of which issue storms and tempests when it is pricked. Above all, Zadig never prided himself on despising women, nor boasted of his conquests over them. Generous as he was, he had no fear of bestowing kindness on the ungrateful, therein following the noble maxim of Zoroaster: *When thou eatest, give something to the dogs, even though they should bite thee.* He was as wise as man can be, for he sought to live with the wise. Instructed in the sciences of the ancient Chaldeans, he was not ignorant of such principles of natural philosophy as were then known, and knew as much of metaphysics as has been known in any age, that is to say, next to nothing. He was firmly persuaded that the year consists of three hundred sixty-five days and a quarter, in spite of the latest philosophy of his time, and that the sun is the center of our system; and when the leading magi told him with contemptuous arrogance that he entertained dangerous opinions, and that it was a proof of hostility to the government to believe that the sun turned on its own axis and that the year had twelve months, he held his peace without showing either anger or disdain.

Zadig, with great riches, and consequently well provided with friends, having health and good looks, a just and well-disciplined mind, and a heart noble and sincere, thought that he might be happy. He was to be married to Semira, a lady whose beauty, birth, and fortune rendered her the first match in Babylon. He felt for her a strong and virtuous attachment, and Semira in her turn loved him passionately. They were close upon the happy moment which was about to unite them, when, walking together towards one of the gates of Babylon, under the palm trees which adorned the banks of the Euphrates, they saw a party of men armed with swords and bows advancing in their direction. They were the satellites of young Orcan, the nephew of a minister of state, whom his uncle's hangers-on had encouraged in the belief that he might do what he liked with impunity. He had none of the graces nor virtues of Zadig; but, fancying he was worth a great deal more, he was provoked at not being preferred to him. This jealousy, which proceeded only from his vanity, made him think that he was desperately in love with Semira, and he determined to carry her off. The ravishers seized her, and in their outrageous violence wounded her, shedding the blood of one so fair that the tigers of Mount Imaus would have melted at the sight of her. She pierced the sky with her lamentations. She cried aloud:

"My dear husband! They are tearing me from him who is the idol of my heart."

Taking no heed of her own danger, it was of her beloved Zadig alone that she thought, who, meanwhile, was defending her with all the force that love and valor could bestow. With the help of only two slaves he put the ravishers to flight, and carried Semira to her home unconscious and covered with blood. On opening her eyes she saw her deliverer, and said:

"O Zadig, I loved you before as my future husband, I love you now as the preserver of my life and honor."

Never was there a heart more deeply moved than that of Semira; never did lips more lovely express sentiments more touching, in words of fire inspired by gratitude for the greatest of benefits and the most tender transports of the most honorable love. Her wound was slight, and was soon cured; but Zadig was hurt more severely, an arrow had struck him near the eye and made a deep wound. Semira's only prayer to Heaven now was that her lover might be healed. Her eyes were bathed in tears night and day; she longed for the moment when those of Zadig might once more be able to gaze on her with delight; but an abscess which attacked the wounded eye gave every cause for alarm. A messenger was sent as far as Memphis for Hermes, the famous physician, who came with a numerous train. He visited the sick man, and declared that he would lose the eye; he even foretold the day and the hour when this unfortunate event would happen.

"If it had been the right eye," said he, "I might have cured it, but injuries to the left eye are incurable."

All Babylon, while bewailing Zadig's fate, admired the profound scientific research of Hermes. Two days afterwards the abscess broke of itself, and Zadig was completely cured. Hermes wrote a book, in which he proved to him that he ought not to have been cured; but Zadig did not read it. As soon as he could venture forth, he prepared to visit her in whom rested his every hope of happiness in life, and for whose sake alone he desired to have eyes. Now Semira had gone into the country three days before, and on his way he learned that this fair lady, after loudly declaring that she had an insurmountable objection to one-eyed people, had just married Orcan the night before. At these tidings he fell senseless, and his anguish brought him to the brink of the grave; he was ill for a long time, but at last reason prevailed over his affliction, and the very atrocity of his treatment furnished him with a source of consolation.

"Since I have experienced," said he, "such cruel caprice from a maiden brought up at the court, I must marry one of the townspeople."

He chose Azora, who came of the best stock and was the best behaved girl in the city. He married her, and lived with her for a month in all the bliss of a most tender union. The only fault he remarked in her was a little giddiness, and a strong tendency to find out that the handsomest young men had always the most intelligence and virtue.

Chapter 2

The Nose

ONE DAY AZORA returned from a walk in a state of vehement indignation and uttering loud exclamations.

"What is the matter with you, my dear wife?" said Zadig; "who can have put you so much out of temper?"

"Alas!" she replied, "you would be as indignant as I, if you had seen the sight which I have just witnessed. I went to console the young widow Cosrou, who two days ago raised a tomb to her young husband beside the stream which forms the boundary of this meadow. She vowed to Heaven, in her grief, that she would dwell beside that tomb as long as the stream flowed by it."

"Well!" said Zadig, "a truly estimable woman, who really loved her husband!"

"Ah!" returned Azora, "if you only knew how she was occupied when I paid her my visit!"

"How then, fair Azora?"

"She was diverting the course of the brook."

Azora gave vent to her feelings in such lengthy invectives, and burst into such violent reproaches against the young widow, that this ostentatious display of virtue was not altogether pleasing to Zadig.

He had a friend named Cador, who was one of those young men in whom his wife found more merit and integrity than in others; Zadig took him into his confidence, and secured his fidelity, as far as possible, by means of a considerable present.

Azora, having passed a couple of days with one of her lady friends in the country, on the third day returned home. The servants, with tears in their eyes, told her that her husband had died quite suddenly the night before, that they had not dared to convey to her such sad news, and that they had just buried Zadig in the tomb of his ancestors at the end of the garden. She wept, and tore her hair, and vowed that she would die. In the evening Cador asked if she would allow him to speak to her, and they wept in company. Next day they wept less, and dined together. Cador informed her that his friend had left him the best part of his property, and gave her to understand that he would deem it the greatest happiness to share his fortune with her. The lady shed tears, was offended, allowed herself to be soothed; the supper lasted longer than the dinner, and they conversed together more confidentially. Azora spoke in praise of the deceased, but admitted that he had faults from which Cador was free.

In the middle of supper, Cador complained of a violent pain in the spleen. The lady, anxious and attentive, caused all the essences on her toilet table to be brought, to try if there might not be some one among them good for affections of the spleen. She was very sorry that the famous Hermes was no longer in Babylon. She even condescended to touch the side where Cador felt such sharp pains.

"Are you subject to this cruel malady?" she asked in a tone of compassion.

"It sometimes brings me to the brink of the grave," answered Cador, "and there is only one remedy which can relieve me: it is to apply to my side the nose of a man who has been only a day or two dead."

"What a strange remedy!" said Azora.

"Not more strange," was his reply, "than the scent-bags of Mr. Arnoult being an antidote to apoplexy."[1]

That reason, joined to the distinguished merit of the young man, at last decided the lady.

"After all," said she, "when my husband shall pass from the world of yesterday into the world of tomorrow over the bridge Chinavar, the angel Azrael will not grant him a passage any the less because his nose will be a little shorter in the second life than in the first."

She then took a razor, and went to her husband's tomb; after she had watered it with her tears, she approached to cut off Zadig's nose, whom she found stretched at full length in the tomb, when he suddenly got up, and, holding his nose with one hand, stopped the razor with the other.

"Madam," said he, "do not cry out so loudly another time against young Cosrou; your intention of cutting off my nose is as bad as that of turning aside a stream."

Chapter 3

The Dog and the Horse

ZADIG FOUND BY experience that the first month of marriage is, as it is written in the book of the Zendavesta, the moon of honey, and that the second is the moon of wormwood. He was some time afterwards obliged to put away Azora, who became too unmanageable to live with, and he sought for happiness in the study of nature.

"There is no delight," he said, "equal to that of a philosopher, who reads in this great book which God has set before our eyes. The truths which he discovers are his own: he nurtures and educates his soul, he lives in peace, he fears no man, and no tender spouse comes to cut off his nose."

Full of these ideas, he retired to a country house on the banks of the Euphrates. There he did not spend his time in calculating how many inches of water flowed in a second under the arches of a bridge, or whether a cubic line of rain fell in the month of the mouse more than in the month of the sheep. He did not contrive how to make silk out of cobwebs, nor porcelain out of broken bottles, but he studied most of all the properties of animals and plants, and soon acquired a sagacity that showed him a thousand differences where other men see nothing but uniformity.

One day, when he was walking near a little wood, he saw one of the queen's eunuchs running to meet him, followed by several officers, who appeared to be in the greatest uneasiness, and who were running hither and thither like men bewildered and searching for some most precious object which they had lost.

"Young man," said the chief eunuch to Zadig, "have you seen the queen's dog?"

Zadig modestly replied: "It is a bitch, not a dog."

"You are right," said the eunuch.

"It is a very small spaniel," added Zadig; "it is not long since she has had a litter of puppies; she is lame in the left forefoot, and her ears are very long."

"You have seen her, then?" said the chief eunuch, quite out of breath.

"No," answered Zadig, "I have never seen her, and never knew that the queen had a bitch."

Just at this very time, by one of those curious coincidences which are not uncommon, the finest horse in the king's stables had broken away from the hands of a groom in the plains of Babylon. The grand huntsman and all the other officers ran after him with as much anxiety as the chief of the eunuchs had displayed in his search after the queen's bitch. The grand huntsman accosted Zadig, and asked him if he had seen the king's horse pass that way.

"It is the horse," said Zadig, "which gallops best; he is five feet high, and has small hoofs; his tail is three and a half feet long; the bosses on his bit are of gold twenty-three carats fine; his shoes are silver of eleven pennyweights."

"Which road did he take? Where is he?" asked the grand huntsman.

"I have not seen him," answered Zadig, "and I have never even heard anyone speak of him."

The grand huntsman and the chief eunuch had no doubt that Zadig had stolen the king's horse and the queen's bitch, so they caused him to be brought before the Assembly of the Grand Desterham, which condemned him to the knout, and to pass the rest of his life in Siberia. Scarcely had the sentence been pronounced, when the horse and the bitch were found. The judges were now under the disagreeable necessity of amending their judgment; but they condemned Zadig to pay four hundred ounces of gold for having said that he had not seen what he had seen. He was forced to pay this fine first, and afterwards he was allowed to plead his cause before the Council of the Grand Desterham, when he expressed himself in the following terms:

"Stars of justice, fathomless gulfs of wisdom, mirrors of truth, ye who have the gravity of lead, the strength of iron, the brilliance of the diamond, and a close affinity with gold, inasmuch as it is permitted me to speak before this august assembly, I swear to you by Ormuzd that I have never seen the queen's respected bitch, nor the sacred horse of the king of kings. Hear all that happened: I was walking towards the little wood where later on I met the venerable eunuch and the most illustrious grand huntsman. I saw on the sand the footprints of an animal, and easily decided that they were those of a little dog. Long and faintly marked furrows, imprinted where the sand was slightly raised between the footprints, told me that it was a bitch whose dugs were drooping and that consequently she must have given birth to young ones only a few days before. Other marks of a different character, showing that the surface of the sand had been constantly grazed on either side of the front paws, informed me that she had very long ears; and, as I observed that the sand was always less deeply indented by one paw than by the other three, I gathered that the bitch belonging to our august queen was a little lame, if I may venture to say so.

"With respect to the horse of the king of kings, you must know that as I was walking along the roads in that same wood, I perceived the marks of a horse's shoes, all at equal distances. 'There,' I said to myself, 'went a horse with a faultless gallop.' The dust upon the trees, where the width of the road was not more than seven feet, was here and there rubbed off on both sides, three feet and a half away from the middle of the road. 'This horse,' said I, 'has a tail three feet and a half long, which, by its movements to right and left, has whisked away the dust.' I saw, where the trees formed a canopy five feet above the ground, leaves lately fallen from the boughs; and I concluded that the horse had touched them, and was therefore five feet high. As to his bit, it must be of gold twenty-three carats fine, for he had rubbed its bosses against a touchstone, the properties of which I had ascertained. Lastly, I inferred from the marks that his shoes left upon stones of another kind, that he was shod with silver of eleven pennyweights in quality."

All the judges marveled at Zadig's deep and subtle discernment, and a report of it even reached the king and queen. Nothing but Zadig was talked of in the antechambers, the presence chamber, and the private closet; and, though several of the magi were of opinion that he ought to be burned as a wizard, the king ordered that he should be released from the fine of four hundred ounces of gold to which he had been condemned. The registrar, the bailiffs, and the attorneys came to his house with great solemnity to restore him his four hundred ounces; they kept back only three hundred and ninety-eight of them for legal expenses, and their servants too claimed their fees.

Zadig saw how very dangerous it sometimes is to show oneself too knowing, and resolved on the next occasion of the kind to say nothing about what he had seen.

Such an opportunity soon occurred. A state prisoner made his escape, and passed under the windows of Zadig's house, who, on being questioned, answered nothing; but it was proved that he had looked out of the window. For this offense he was condemned to pay five hundred ounces of gold, and he thanked his judges for their leniency, according to the custom of Babylon.

"Good Heavens!" said Zadig to himself. "What a pity it is when one takes a walk in a wood through which the queen's bitch and the king's horse have passed! How dangerous it is to stand at a window! And how difficult it is to be happy in this life!"

Chapter 4

The Envious Man

ZADIG SOUGHT CONSOLATION in philosophy and friendship for the unkindness with which fortune had treated him. In one of the suburbs of Babylon he had a house tastefully furnished, where he had gathered all the arts and pleasures that were worthy of a gentleman. In the morning his library was open to all men of learning; in the evening his table was surrounded by good company. But he soon discovered what danger there is in entertaining the learned. A hot dispute arose over a law of Zoroaster, which prohibited the eating of a griffin.

"How can a griffin be forbidden," said some, "if no such creature exists?"

"It must exist," said the others, "since Zoroaster forbids it to be eaten."

Zadig endeavored to bring them to an agreement by saying:

"If there are griffins, let us refrain from eating them; and if there are none, there will be all the less danger of our doing so. Thus, in either case alike, Zoroaster will be obeyed."

A learned scholar who had composed thirteen volumes on the properties of the griffin, and who was moreover a great magician, lost no time in bringing an accusation against Zadig before an archimagian named Yebor,[2] the most foolish of the Chaldeans, and consequently the most fanatical. This man would fain have impaled Zadig for the greater glory of the Sun, and would have recited the breviary of Zoroaster in a more complacent tone of voice for having done it; but Zadig's friend Cador (one friend is worth more than a hundred priests) sought out old Yebor, and addressed him thus:

"Long live the Sun and the griffins! Take good heed that you do no harm to Zadig; he is a saint; he keeps griffins in his back yard, and abstains from eating them; and his accuser is a heretic who dares to maintain that rabbits have cloven feet and are not unclean."

"In that case," said Yebor, shaking his bald head, "Zadig must be impaled for having thought wrongly about griffins, and the other for having spoken wrongly about rabbits."

Cador settled the matter by means of a maid of honor, who had borne Yebor a child, and who was held in high esteem in the college of the magi. No one was impaled, though a good many of the doctors murmured thereat, and prophesied the downfall of Babylon in consequence.

Zadig exclaimed: "On what does happiness depend! Everybody in this world persecutes me, even beings that do not exist."

He cursed all men of learning, and determined to live henceforth only in the best society. He invited to his house the most distinguished men and the most charming women in Babylon; he gave elegant suppers, often preceded by concerts, and enlivened by interesting conversation, from which he knew how to banish that straining after a display of wit which is the surest way to have none and to mar the most brilliant company. Neither the choice of his friends, nor that of his dishes, was prompted by vanity; for in everything he preferred being to seeming, and thereby he attracted to himself the real respect to which he made no claim.

Opposite Zadig's house lived Arimaze, a person whose depraved soul was painted on his coarse countenance.[3] He was consumed with malice, and puffed up with pride, and, to crown all, he set up for being a wit and was only a bore. Having never been able to succeed in the world, he took his revenge by railing at it. In spite of his riches, he had some trouble in getting flatterers to flock to his house. The noise of the carriages entering Zadig's gates of an evening annoyed him, and the sound of his praises irritated him yet more. He sometimes went to Zadig's parties and sat down at his table without being invited, where he spoiled all the enjoyment of the company, just as the harpies are said to infect whatever food they touch. One day a lady whom he was anxious to entertain, instead of accepting his invitation, went to sup with Zadig. Another day, when he was talking with Zadig in the palace, they came across a minister who asked Zadig to supper without asking Arimaze. The most inveterate hatreds are often founded on causes quite as trivial. This person, who went by the name of "the Envious man" in Babylon, wished to ruin Zadig because people called him "the Happy man." Opportunities for doing harm are found a hundred times a day, and an opportunity for doing good occurs once a year, as Zoroaster has observed.

On one occasion the Envious man went to Zadig's house and found him walking in his garden with two friends and a lady, to whom he was addressing frequent compliments, without any intention other than that of making himself agreeable. The conversation turned upon a war, which the king had just brought to a prosperous termination, against the prince of Hyrcania, his vassal. Zadig, who had displayed his valor during the short campaign, had much to say in praise of the king, and still more in praise of the lady. He took out his notebook, and wrote down four lines, which he made on the spur of the moment, and which he gave to his fair companion to read. His friends entreated him to be allowed a sight of them; but his modesty, or rather a natural regard for his reputation, made him refuse. He knew that such impromptu verses are never of any value except in the eyes of her in whose honor they have been composed, so he tore in two the leaf on which he had just written them, and threw the pieces into a thicket of roses, where his friends looked for them in vain. A shower came on, and they betook themselves indoors. The Envious man, who remained in the garden, searched so diligently that he found one fragment of the leaf, which had been torn in such a way that the halves of each line that was left made sense, and even a rhymed verse, in shorter meter than the original. But by an accident still more strange, these short lines were found to contain the most opprobrious libel against the king. They read thus:

> "By heinous crimes
> Set on the throne,
> In peaceful times
> One foe alone."

The Envious man was happy for the first time in his life, for he had in his hands the means of destroying a virtuous and amiable man. Full of such cruel joy, he caused this lampoon written by Zadig's own hand to be brought to the king's notice, who ordered Zadig to be sent to prison, together with his two friends and the lady. His trial was soon over, nor did his judges deign to hear what he had to say for himself. When he was brought up to receive sentence, the Envious man crossed his path, and told him in a loud voice that his verses were good for nothing. Zadig did not pride himself on being a fine poet, but he was in despair at being condemned as guilty of high treason, and at seeing so fair a lady and his two friends kept in prison for a crime that he had never committed. He was not allowed to speak, because his notebook spoke for him. Such was the law of Babylon. He was then forced to go to his execution through a crowd of inquisitive spectators, not one of whom dared to commiserate him, but who rushed forward in order to scrutinize his countenance, and to see whether he was likely to die with a good grace. His relations alone were distressed; for they were not to be his heirs. Three quarters of his estate were confiscated for the king's benefit, and the Envious man profited by the other quarter.

Just as he was preparing for death, the king's parrot escaped from its perch, and alighted in Zadig's garden, on a thicket of roses. A peach had been carried thither by the wind from a tree hard by, and it had fallen on a piece of writing paper, to which it had stuck. The bird took up both the peach and the paper, and laid them on the monarch's knees. The king, whose curiosity was excited, read some words which made no sense, and which appeared to be the ends of four lines of verse. He loved poetry, and princes who love the muses never find time hangs heavy on their hands. His parrot's adventure set him thinking. The queen, who remembered what had been written on the fragment of the leaf from Zadig's notebook, had it brought to her.

Both pieces were put side by side, and were found to fit together exactly. The verses then read as Zadig had made them:

> "By heinous crimes I saw the earth alarm'd,
> Set on the throne one king all evil curbs;
> In peaceful times now only Love is arm'd,
> One foe alone the timid heart disturbs."

The king immediately commanded that Zadig should be brought before him, and that his two friends and the fair lady should be let out of prison. Zadig prostrated himself with his face to the ground at their majesties' feet, asked their pardon most humbly for having made such poor rhymes, and spoke with so much grace, wit, and good sense, that the king and queen desired to see him again. He came again accordingly, and won still greater favor. All the property of the Envious man who had accused him unjustly was given to Zadig, but he restored it all, and the Envious man was touched, but only with the joy of not losing his wealth after all. The king's esteem for Zadig increased every day. He made him share all his pleasures, and consulted him in all matters of business. The queen regarded him from that time with a tender complacency that might become dangerous to herself, to her royal consort, to Zadig, and to the whole State. Zadig began to think that it is not so difficult after all to be happy.

Chapter 5
The Prize of Generosity

THE TIME HAD now arrived for celebrating a high festival, which recurred every five years. It was the custom at Babylon, at the end of such a period, to announce in a public and solemn manner the name of that citizen who had done the most generous act during the interval. The grandees and the magi were the arbitrators. The chief satrap, who had the city under his charge, made known the most noble deeds that had been performed under his government. The election was made by vote, and the king pronounced judgment. People came to this festival from the farthest corners of the earth, and the successful candidate received from the monarch's hands a cup of gold decorated with precious stones, the king addressing him in these terms:

"Receive this reward of generosity, and may the gods grant me many subjects who resemble you."

The memorable day then was come, and the king appeared upon his throne, surrounded by grandees, magi, and deputies, sent by all nations to these games, where glory was to be gained, not by the swiftness of horses nor by strength of body, but by virtue. The chief satrap proclaimed with a loud voice the actions that might entitle their authors to this inestimable prize. He said nothing about the magnanimity with which Zadig had restored all his fortune to the Envious man; that was not considered an action worthy of disputing the prize.

First, he presented a judge who, after having given judgment against a citizen in an important lawsuit, under a mistake for which he was in no way responsible, had given him all his own property, which was equal in value to what the other had lost.

He next brought forward a young man, who, being over head and ears in love with a damsel to whom he was engaged to be married, had resigned her to a friend who was nearly dying for love of her, and had moreover resigned the dowry as well as the damsel.

Then he introduced a soldier, who in the Hyrcanian war had given a still nobler example of generosity. Some of the enemy's troops were laying hands on his mistress, and he was defending her from them, when he was told that another party of Hyrcanians, a few paces off, were carrying away his mother. With tears he left his mistress, and ran to rescue his mother; and when he returned to the object of his love, he found her dying. He was on the point of slaying himself, but when his mother pointed out that she had no one but him to whom she could look for succor, he was courageous enough to endure to live on.

The arbitrators were inclined to give the prize to this soldier; but the king interposed, and said:

"This man's conduct and that of the others is praiseworthy, but it does not astonish me; whereas yesterday Zadig did a thing that made me marvel. Some days before, my minister and favorite, Coreb, had incurred my displeasure and been disgraced. I uttered violent complaints against him, and all my courtiers assured me that I was not half severe enough; each vied with his neighbor in saying as much evil as he could of Coreb. I asked Zadig what he thought of him, and he dared to say a word in his favor. I am free to confess that I have heard of instances in our history of men atoning for a mistake by the sacrifice of their goods, giving up a mistress, or preferring a mother to a sweetheart, but I have never read of a courtier speaking a good word for a minister in disgrace, against whom his sovereign was bitterly incensed. I award twenty thousand pieces of gold to each of those whose generous acts have been recounted; but I award the cup to Zadig."

"Sire," said Zadig, "it is Your Majesty alone who deserves the cup for having done a deed of unprecedented magnanimity, in that, being a king, you were not angry with your slave when he ran counter to your passion."

The king and Zadig were regarded with equal admiration. The judge who had given away his fortune, the lover who allowed his friend to marry his mistress, and the soldier who had preferred his mother's safety to that of his sweetheart, received at the monarch's hands the presents he had assigned, and saw their names written in the Book of the Generous, but Zadig had the cup. The king gained the reputation of a good prince, which he did not keep long. The day was celebrated with feasts that lasted longer than the law directed, and its memory is still preserved in Asia. Zadig said:

"At last, then, I am happy." But he was deceived.

Chapter 6
The Minister

THE KING HAD lost his prime minister, and chose Zadig to fill his place. All the fair ladies in Babylon applauded the choice; for since the foundation of the empire there had never been known such a young minister. All the courtiers were offended; and the Envious man spat blood on hearing the news, while his nose swelled to an enormous size. Zadig, having thanked the king and queen, proceeded to thank the parrot also.

"Beautiful bird," he said, "it is you who have saved my life, and made me prime minister: the bitch and the horse belonging to Their Majesties did me much harm, but you have done me good. On what slight threads do human destinies depend! But," added he, "a happiness so strangely acquired will, perhaps, soon pass by."

"Ay," replied the parrot.

Zadig was startled at the response; but, being a good naturalist, and not believing that parrots were prophets, he soon recovered himself.

Applying all his energies to the duties of his office, he made everybody feel the sacred power of the laws, but made no one feel the weight of his dignity. He did not interfere with the free expression of opinion in the divan, and each vizier was welcome to hold his own without displeasing him. When he acted as judge in any matter, it was not he who pronounced sentence, it was the law. But when the law was too harsh, he tempered its severity, and when there were no laws to meet the case, his sense of equity supplied him with decisions that might have been taken for those of Zoroaster.

It is from Zadig that the nations of the world have received the grand maxim: "It is better that a guilty man should be acquitted than that an innocent one should be condemned." He held that laws were made as much for the sake of helping as of intimidating the people.

His chief skill lay in revealing the truth which all men try to darken. From the very beginning of his administration he put this great talent to good use. A famous merchant of Babylon had died in India and made his two sons heirs to equal portions of his estate, after having given their sister in marriage; and he left a present of thirty thousand gold pieces to that one of his two sons who should be judged to have shown the greater love towards him. The elder built him a tomb, the second increased his sister's dowry with a part of his own inheritance. Everybody said: "It is the elder son who has the greater love for his father, the younger loves his sister better; the thirty thousand pieces belong to the elder."

Zadig sent for the two brothers, one after the other. He said to the elder:

"Your father is not dead; he has been cured of his last illness, and is returning to Babylon."

"God be praised!" answered the young man, "but his tomb has cost me a large sum of money."

Zadig then said the same thing to the younger brother.

"God be praised!" answered he; "I will restore to my father all that I have, but I hope that he will leave my sister what I have given her."

"You shall restore nothing," said Zadig, "and you shall have the thirty thousand pieces; it is you who love your father best."

A very rich young lady had promised her hand to two magi, and, after having received a course of instruction for some months from each of them, found herself likely to become a mother. Both still wishing to marry her, she said she would take for her husband the one who had put her in a position to present the empire with a citizen.

"It is I who have done that good work," said one of them.

"It is I who have had that privilege," said the other.

"Well," answered she, "I will recognize that one as the father of the child who can give him the best education."

She was brought to bed of a son. Each of the two magi wished to bring it up, and the case was referred to Zadig, who summoned the magi to his presence.

"What will you teach your pupil?" he asked of the first.

"I will instruct him," said the learned professor, "in the eight parts of speech, in logic, astrology, demonology, the difference between substance and accident, abstract and concrete, the doctrine of the monads and the pre-established harmony."[4]

"For my part," said the other, "I will endeavor to render him just and worthy of having friends."

Zadig exclaimed: "Whether you are his father or not, you shall marry his mother."

Day after day complaints reached court of the governor of Media, whose name was Irax. He was a high and mighty personage, not a bad fellow at bottom, but spoiled by vanity and self-indulgence. He seldom suffered anyone to speak to him, and never to contradict him. Peacocks are not more conceited than he was, nor doves more voluptuous, nor turtles more indolent; every breath he drew was devoted to vainglory and false pleasures. Zadig undertook to reform him.

He sent him, in the king's name, a skillful musician with a dozen singers and two dozen fiddlers, also a butler with half a dozen cooks and four chamberlains, who were never to leave him alone. By the king's orders the following ceremonies were strictly observed, and this is how matters were carried on.

The first day, as soon as the pleasure-loving Irax was awake, the musical conductor entered his chamber followed by the singers and fiddlers: a cantata was sung which lasted two hours, and every three minutes there was this refrain:

> "Whose merits e'er attain'd such height?
>   Who with such grace was e'er endow'd?
> Has not his Highness every right
>   To feel self-satisfied and proud?"

After this cantata was performed, one of the chamberlains made him a speech, three quarters of an hour long, in which he praised him expressly for all those good qualities in which he was most deficient. The oration finished, he was escorted to the table to the sound of musical instruments. The dinner lasted three hours; whenever he opened his mouth to speak, the first chamberlain said: "Whatever he says will be right." Scarcely had he spoken four words, when the second chamberlain would exclaim: "He is right." The two other chamberlains burst into fits of laughter at all the witticisms which Irax uttered, or which they attributed to him. After dinner he was favored with a repetition of the cantata.

This first day seemed to him delightful; he thought that the king of kings was honoring him according to his deserts. The second appeared a little less agreeable, the third palled upon him considerably, the fourth was intolerable, and the fifth absolute torture. At last, rather than hear the continual refrain:

> "Has not his Highness every right
> To feel self-satisfied and proud?"

rather than hear the perpetual assurance that whatever he said was right, rather than be harangued every day at the same hour, he wrote to the court entreating the king to be good enough to recall his chamberlains, his musicians, and his butler; and he promised to be less vain and more industrious in future. He was henceforth less tolerant of flattery, gave fewer entertainments, and was all the happier; for, as the Sadder[5] has said:

> "Continual pleasure is no pleasure."

Chapter 7

Settling Disputes and Giving Audience

THUS IT WAS that Zadig daily showed the shrewdness of his intellect and the goodness of his heart. He was admired, yet he was also loved. He passed for the most fortunate of men; all the empire resounded with his name, all the women ogled him, and all the citizens extolled his justice, the men of science regarded him as their oracle, and even the priests confessed that he knew more than the old archimagian Yebor. Far from wishing to prosecute him for his opinions on the subject of griffins, they believed only what seemed credible to him.

Now there was a great controversy in babylon which had lasted fifteen hundred years and had divided the empire into two bigoted sects: one maintained that the temple of Mithras should never be entered except with the left foot foremost; the other held this practice in abomination, and always entered with the right foot first. The rival sects waited impatiently for the day on which the solemn feast of the holy fire was to be held, to know which side would be favored by Zadig. All had their eyes fixed on his two feet, and the whole city was in agitation and suspense. Zadig leaped into the temple with both his feet together, and afterwards proved in an eloquent discourse that the God of heaven and earth, who is no respecter of persons, cares no more for the left leg than for the right. The Envious man and his wife contended that there were not enough figures of speech in his discourse, that he had not made the mountains and hills skip about freely enough.

"He is dry and wants imagination," they said; "one does not see the ocean fly before him, nor the stars fall, nor the sun melt like wax; he lacks the fine oriental style."

Zadig was content with having the style of a reasonable man. He was a favorite with all classes, not because he was in the right road, nor because he was reasonable, nor even because he was amiable, but because he was grand vizier.

He also happily put an end to the hot dispute between the white and the black magi. The white asserted that it was impious, when praying to God, to turn towards the east in winter; the black were confident that God abhorred the prayers of those who turned towards the west in summer. Zadig directed that men should turn to whatever quarter of the compass they pleased.

He likewise found out the secret of dispatching all his business, both public and private, in the morning, and he employed the rest of the day in providing Babylon with refined entertainments. He caused tragedies to be presented which moved the audience to tears, and comedies that made them laugh; a custom which had long passed out of fashion, and which he had the good taste to revive. He did not pretend to know more about their art than the actors themselves; he rewarded them with gifts and distinctions, and was not secretly jealous of their talents. In the evenings he diverted the king much, and the queen still more.

"A great minister!" said the king.

"A charming minister!" said the queen.

Both of them agreed that it would have been a thousand pities if Zadig had been hanged.

Never was statesman in office obliged to give so many audiences to the ladies. The greater number came to speak to him about no business in particular for the sake of having particular business with him. The wife of the Envious man presented herself among the first; she swore by Mithras and the Zendavesta and the holy fire that she detested the conduct of her husband; then she told him in confidence that this husband of hers was jealous and treated her brutally, and gave him to understand that the gods punished him by refusing him the precious effects of that holy fire whereby alone man is made like the immortals. She ended by dropping her garter. Zadig picked it up with his customary politeness, but did not offer to fasten it again round the lady's knee, and this little fault, if it can be considered such, was the cause of the most dreadful misfortunes. Zadig thought no more about the incident, but the Envious man's wife thought about it a great deal.

Other ladies continued to present themselves every day. The secret annals of Babylon assert that he yielded to temptation on only one occasion, but that he was astonished to find that he enjoyed his mistress without pleasure, and that his mind was distracted even in the midst of the tenderest embraces. The fair one to whom he gave, almost unconsciously, these tokens of his favor was a lady in waiting to Queen Astarte. This amorous daughter of Babylon consoled herself for his coldness by saying to herself:

"That man must have a prodigious amount of business in his head, since his thoughts are absorbed with it even when he is making love."

Zadig happened at a moment when many people say nothing and others only utter terms of endearment, to suddenly exclaim: "The queen!" The fair Babylonian fancied that he had at last recovered his wits at a happy moment, and that he was addressing her as his queen. But Zadig, still absent-minded, proceeded to utter the name of Astarte. The lady, who in this agreeable situation interpreted everything in a flattering sense, imagined that he meant to say: "You are more beautiful than Queen Astarte." She left the seraglio of Zadig with magnificent presents, and went to relate her adventure to the Envious woman, who was her intimate friend. The latter was cruelly piqued at the preference shown to the other.

"He did not even condescend," said she, "to replace this garter which I have here, and which I will never use again."

"Oh!" said her more fortunate friend, "you wear the same garters as the queen! Do you get them from the same maker?"

The Envious woman fell into a brown study, and made no reply, but went and consulted her husband, the Envious man.

Meanwhile Zadig became aware of his constant absence of mind whenever he gave an audience or administered justice; he did not know to what to attribute it; it was his only subject of annoyance.

He had a dream, in which he seemed to be lying at first on a heap of dry herbs, among which were some prickly ones which made him uncomfortable, and that afterwards he reposed luxuriously upon a bed of roses, out of which glided a snake that wounded him in the heart with its pointed and poisoned tongue.[6]

"Alas!" said he, "I lay a long time on those dry and prickly herbs; I am now on the bed of roses; but who will be the serpent?"

Chapter 8
Jealousy

ZADIG'S ILL LUCK arose out of his very happiness, and was mainly due to his merits. He had daily interviews with the king and with Astarte, his august consort. The charm of his conversation was doubled by that desire to please which is to the mind what ornaments are to personal beauty; his youth and graceful manners insensibly made an impression upon Astarte, of the strength of which she was not at first aware. Her passion grew up in the bosom of innocence. Astarte gave herself up without scruple and without fear to the pleasure of seeing and hearing a man who was so dear to her husband and to the State; she never ceased singing his praises to the king; she was perpetually speaking about him to her women, who even went beyond her in their commendations; everything served to fix more deeply in her heart the arrow of which she was unconscious. She bestowed presents upon Zadig, into which more love making entered than she supposed; she meant to speak to him as a queen satisfied with his services, but the expressions she used were sometimes those of a women of tender sensibility.

Astarte was much more beautiful than that Semira who had such a detestation of one-eyed men, or that other woman who had intended to cut off her husband's nose. Astarte's familiar manner, her soft speeches at which she began to blush, her eyes which, despite her efforts to turn them away, were ever fixed upon his own, kindled in Zadig's heart a fire which filled him with astonishment. He fought against his feelings; he called to his aid the philosophy which had never before failed him; he drew from it nothing but a clearer perception of his folly, and received no relief. Duty, gratitude, and outraged majesty presented themselves to his view as so many avenging deities; he struggled, and he triumphed; but this victory, which had to be repeated every moment, cost him groans and tears. He no longer dared to address the queen with that delightful freedom which had had such charms for both of them; a cloud overshadowed his eyes; his conversation was constrained and abrupt; his eyes were downcast, and when, in spite of himself, they turned towards Astarte, they encountered those of the queen moistened with tears from which there shot forth arrows of flame. They seemed to say to each other:

"Our adoration is mutual, yet we are afraid to love; we are both consumed with a fire which we condemn."

When Zadig left her side it was with bewilderment and despair, his heart oppressed with a burden which he was no longer able to support: in the violence of his agitation he let his friend Cador penetrate his secret, like a man who, after having endured the most excruciating pains, at last makes his malady known by a cry which a keener spasm than any before wrings from him, and by the cold sweat which pours over his forehead.

Cador addressed him as follows:

"I have already divined the feelings that you would fain hide from yourself; the passions have symptoms which cannot be misinterpreted. Judge, my dear Zadig, since I have been able to read your heart, whether the king is not likely to discover there a sentiment that may give him serious offense. He has no other fault but that of being the most jealous of men. You resist your passion with more vigor than the queen can contend against hers, because you are a philosopher, and because you are Zadig. Astarte is a woman; she lets her looks speak for her with all the more imprudence that she does not yet believe herself blameworthy. Assured of her innocence, she unfortunately neglects appearances which it is necessary to observe. I shall tremble for her so long as she has nothing wherewith to reproach herself. If you came to a common understanding, you would be able to throw dust into all eyes; a growing passion, forcibly checked, gives evident tokens of its existence; but love when gratified can easily conceal itself."

Zadig shuddered at the suggestion of betraying the king, his benefactor; and he was never more faithful to his prince than when guilty of an involuntary crime against him. Meanwhile the queen pronounced the name of Zadig so often, she blushed so deeply as she uttered it, she was sometimes so animated, and at other times so confused when she addressed him in the king's presence, and she was seized with so profound a fit of abstraction whenever he went away, that the king began to be alarmed. He believed all that he saw, and imagined all that he did not see. He particularly remarked that his wife's slippers were blue, and that Zadig's slippers were blue; that his wife's ribbons were yellow, and that Zadig's cap was yellow.

Terrible indications, these, to a prince of such delicate sensibility! Suspicion soon became certainty in his envenomed mind.

All the slaves of kings and queens are so many spies over their hearts. It was soon discovered that Astarte was tender and that Moabdar was jealous. The Envious man got his wife to send the king her garter, which was like the queen's; and, to make the matter worse, this garter was blue. The monarch thought of nothing now but how to take his revenge. One night he determined to poison the queen, and to have Zadig strangled as soon as it was light. The order was given to a merciless eunuch, the usual executioner of his vengeance. Now there happened to be in the king's chamber at this time a little dwarf, who was dumb but not deaf. He was allowed to wander about when and where he pleased, and, like a domestic animal, was oftentimes a witness of what passed in the strictest privacy. This little mute was much attached to the queen and Zadig, and he heard with no less surprise than horror the order given for their death. But what could he do to prevent this frightful order, which was to be carried out within a few hours? He did not know how to write, but he had learned how to paint, and was particularly skillful in making likenesses. He spent part of the night in portraying what he wished the queen to understand. His sketch represented in one corner of the picture the king in a furious rage, giving orders to his eunuch; a blue bowstring and a cup on a table, with garters and yellow ribbons; the queen in the middle of the picture, expiring in the arms of her women, and Zadig lying strangled at her feet. A rising sun was represented on the horizon to indicate that this horrible execution was to take place at the earliest glimpse of dawn. As soon as this task was finished he ran to one of Astarte's women, awoke her, and made her understand that she must take the picture that very instant to the queen.

In the middle of the night someone knocked at Zadig's door; he was roused from sleep, and a note from the queen was given him; he doubted whether or not it were a dream, and opened the letter with a trembling hand. What was his surprise, and who could express the consternation and despair with which he was overwhelmed, when he read these words: "Fly, this very moment, or you will be seized and put to death! Fly, Zadig; I command you in the name of our love and of my yellow ribbons. I have done nothing wrong, but I foresee that I am going to die like a criminal."

Zadig, who had scarcely strength enough to speak, sent for Cador, and then, without a word, gave him the letter. Cador forced him to obey its injunction, and to set out immediately for Memphis.

"If you venture to go in search of the queen," said he, "you will only hasten her death; if you speak to the king, that step again will lead to her destruction. Her fate shall be my care; do you follow your own. I will spread the report that you have taken the road to India. I will soon come and find you out, when I will tell you all that shall have passed at Babylon."

Cador, without a moment's delay, had two of the swiftest dromedaries brought to a private postern of the palace, and made Zadig mount one of them; he had to be carried, for he was almost ready to expire. Only one servant accompanied him, and soon Cador, plunged in astonishment and grief, lost sight of his friend.

The illustrious fugitive, when he arrived at the brow of a hill which commanded a view of Babylon, turned his gaze towards the queen's palace, and fainted. He recovered his senses only to shed tears and to wish that he was dead. At last, after having occupied his thoughts awhile with the deplorable fate of the most amiable of women and the best of queens, he returned for a moment to himself, and exclaimed:

"What, then, is human life? O virtue! Of what use hast thou been to me? Two women have basely deceived me, and the third, who is innocent and is more beautiful than the others, is about to die! All the good that I have done has always brought upon me a curse, and I have been raised to the height of grandeur only to fall down the most horrible precipice of misfortune. If I had been wicked, like so many others, I should be happy like them."

Overwhelmed with these gloomy reflections, his eyes shrouded with a veil of sorrow, the paleness of death on his countenance, and his soul sunk in the depths of a dark despair, he continued his journey towards Egypt.

Chapter 9

The Beaten Woman

ZADIG DIRECTED HIS course by the stars. The constellation of Orion and the bright star of Sirius guided him towards the harbor of Canopus. He marveled at those vast globes of light, which appear only like feeble sparks to our eyes, while the earth, which is in reality nothing more than an imperceptible point in nature, appears to our covetous eyes something grand and noble. He then pictured to himself men as they really are, insects devouring one another on a little atom of clay. This true image seemed to annihilate his misfortunes, by making him realize the insignificance of his own existence and that of Babylon itself. His soul launched forth into the infinitude of space, detached from the operation of the senses, and contemplated the unchangeable order of the universe. But when, afterwards returning to himself and once more looking into his own heart, he thought how Astarte was perhaps already dead for his sake, the universe vanished from his eyes, and he saw nothing in all nature save Astarte dying and Zadig miserable. As he gave himself up to this alternate flow of sublime philosophy and overwhelming grief, he approached the confines of Egypt; and his faithful servant was already in the first village, looking out for a lodging. Zadig was, meanwhile, walking towards the gardens which skirted the village, and saw, not far from the highroad, a woman in great distress, who was calling out to heaven and earth for succor, and a man who was following her in a furious rage. He had already reached her before Zadig could do so, and the woman was clasping his knees, while the man overwhelmed her with blows and reproaches. He judged from the Egyptian's violence and from the repeated prayers for forgiveness which the lady uttered, that he was jealous and she unfaithful; but after he had closely regarded the woman, who was of enchanting beauty, and who, moreover, bore a little resemblance to the unhappy Astarte, he felt moved with compassion towards her, and with horror towards the Egyptian.

"Help me!" she cried to Zadig in a voice choked with sobs; "deliver me out of the hands of this most barbarous man, and save my life!"

Hearing these cries, Zadig ran and threw himself between her and the barbarian; and having some knowledge of the Egyptian tongue, he addressed him in that language, and said:

"If you have any humanity, I entreat you to respect beauty and weakness. How can you illtreat so cruelly such a masterpiece of nature as lies there at your feet, with no protection but her tears?"

"Ah, ha!" answered the man, more enraged than ever; "then you are another of her lovers! And on you too I must take revenge."

Saying these words, he left the lady, whom he had been holding by the hair with one hand, and, seizing his lance, made an attempt to run the stranger through with it. But he, being cool and composed, easily avoided the thrust of one who was beside himself with rage, and caught hold of the lance near the iron point with which it was armed. The one tried to draw it back, while the other tried to wrench it out of his hand, so that it was broken between the two.

The Egyptian drew his sword, Zadig did the same, and they forthwith attacked each other; the former dealing a hundred blows in quick succession, the latter skillfully warding them off. The lady, seated on a piece of turf, readjusted her headdress, and looked calmly on. The Egyptian was stronger than his antagonist, Zadig was the more dexterous. The latter fought like a man whose arm was guided by his head, the former like a madman who in blind frenzy delivered random strokes. Zadig, attacking him in his turn, disarmed his adversary; and while the Egyptian, rendered still more furious, tried to throw himself upon him, the other seized him with a tight grip, and threw him on the ground; then, holding his sword to his breast, he offered to give him his life. The Egyptian, transported with rage, drew his dagger, and therewith wounded Zadig, at the very instant that the conqueror was granting him pardon. Provoked beyond endurance, Zadig plunged his sword into the other's heart. The Egyptian uttered a horrible yell, and died struggling violently. Then Zadig advanced towards the lady, and said in a respectful tone:

"He forced me to kill him; you I have avenged, and delivered out of the hands of the most outrageous man I ever saw. What will you have me do for you now, madam?"

"To die, scoundrel," she replied; "to die! You have killed my lover; I would that I were able to tear out your heart."

"Truly, madam, you had a strange sort of lover in him," returned Zadig; "he was beating you with all his might, and he wanted to have my life because you implored me to help you."

"I wish he was beating me still," answered the lady, giving vent to loud lamentation; "I well deserved it, and gave him good cause for jealousy. Would to heaven that he were beating me and that you were in his place!"

Zadig, more surprised and indignant than he had ever been before in his life, said to her:

"Madam, beautiful as you are, you deserve to have me beat you in my turn for your unreasonable behavior, but I shall not take the trouble."

So saying, he remounted his camel, and advanced towards the village. He had hardly proceeded a few steps when he turned back at the clatter of four messengers riding post haste from Babylon. One of them, seeing the woman, exclaimed:

"That is the very person! She resembles the description that was given us."

They did not encumber themselves with the dead body, but forth-with caught hold of the lady, who never ceased calling out to Zadig:

"Help me once more, generous stranger! I beg your pardon for having reproached you: help me, and I will be yours till death."

Zadig no longer felt any desire to fight on her behalf.

"Apply to someone else," he answered, "you will not entrap me again."

Moreover he was wounded and bleeding; he had need of help himself; and the sight of the four Babylonians, probably sent by King Moabdar, filled him with uneasiness. So he hastened towards the village, unable to imagine why four messengers from Babylon should come to take this Egyptian woman, but still more astonished at the conduct of the lady.

Chapter 10

Slavery

As HE ENTERED the Egyptian village, he found himself surrounded by the people. Everyone was crying out:

"This is the fellow who carried off the lovely Missouf, and who has just murdered Cletofis!"

"Gentlemen," said he, "may Heaven preserve me from carrying off your lovely Missouf! She is too capricious for me; and with regard to Cletofis, I have not murdered him, I only fought against him in self-defense. He wanted to kill me because I had asked him most humbly to pardon the lovely Missouf, whom he was beating unmercifully. I am a stranger come to seek a refuge in Egypt; and it is not likely that, in coming to claim your protection, I should begin by carrying off a woman and murdering a man."

The Egyptians were at that time just and humane. The people conducted Zadig to the court-house. They began by getting his wound dressed, and then they questioned him and his servant sepa-rately, in order to learn the truth. They came to the conclusion that Zadig was not a murderer; but he was found guilty of homicide, and the law condemned him to be a slave. His two camels were sold for the benefit of the village; all the gold that he carried was distributed among the inhabitants; his person was exposed for sale in the marketplace, as well as that of his fellow traveler. An Arab merchant, named Setoc, made the highest bid for him; but the serving-man, as more fit for hard work, was sold at a much higher price than the master. There was no comparison, it was thought, between the two men; so Zadig became a slave of inferior position to his own servant. They were fastened together with a chain, which was passed round their ankles, and in that state they followed the Arab merchant to his house. Zadig, on the way, tried to console his servant, and exhorted him to be patient; and, according to his custom, he made some general reflections on human life.

"I see," he said, "that my unhappy fate has spread its shadow over yours. Hitherto at every turn I have met with strange reverses. I have been condemned to pay a fine for having seen traces of a passing bitch; I thought I was going to be impaled on account of a griffin; I have been sent to execution because I made some complimentary verses on the king; I was on the point of being strangled because the queen had yellow ribbons; and here am I a slave along with you, because a brute of a man chose to beat his mistress. Come, let us not lose courage; all this perhaps will come to an end. It must needs be that Arab merchants should have slaves; and why should not I be one as well as another, since I also am a man? This merchant will not be unmerciful; he must treat his slaves well, if he wishes to make good use of them."

Thus he spoke, but in the depths of his heart he was thinking only of the fate of the queen of Babylon.

Setoc the merchant started, two days afterwards, for Arabia Deserta, with his slaves and his camels. His tribe dwelt near the desert of Horeb, the way to which was long and dangerous. Setoc, on the journey, took greater care of the servant than of the master, because the former could load the camels much better, and any little distinction that was made between them was in his favor.

A camel died two days before they expected to reach Horeb, and its load was distributed among the men, so that each back had its burden, Zadig's among the rest. Setoc laughed to see how all his slaves were bent almost double as they walked. Zadig took the liberty of explaining to him the reason, and gave him some instruction in the laws of equilibrium. The astonished merchant began to regard him with other eyes. Zadig, seeing that he had excited his master's curiosity, increased it by teaching him many things that had a direct bearing on his business, such as the specific gravity of metals and commodities in equal bulk, the properties of several useful animals, and the way in which those might be rendered useful which were not naturally so, until Setoc thought him a sage. He now gave Zadig the preference over his comrade, whom he had before esteemed so highly. He treated him well, and had no reason to repent of it.

Having reached his tribe, the first thing Setoc did was to demand repayment of five hundred ounces of silver from a Jew to whom he had lent them in the presence of two witnesses; but these two witnesses were dead, and the Jew, assured that there was no proof of the debt, appropriated the merchant's money and thanked God for having given him the opportunity of cheating an Arab. Setoc confided his trouble to Zadig, who was now his adviser in everything.

"In what place was it," asked Zadig, "that you lent these five hundred ounces to the infidel?"

"On a large stone near Mount Horeb," answered the merchant.

"What kind of man is your debtor?" said Zadig.

"A regular rogue," returned Setoc.

"But I mean, is he hasty or deliberate, cautious or imprudent?"

"Of all bad payers," said Setoc, "he is the hastiest man I ever knew."

"Well," pursued Zadig, "allow me to plead your cause before the judge."

In the end he summoned the Jew to take his trial, and thus addressed the judge:

"Pillar of the throne of equity, I come here to claim from this man, in my master's name, repayment of five hundred ounces of silver which he will not restore."

"Have you witnesses?" asked the judge.

"No, they are dead; but there still remains a large stone upon which the money was counted out; and, if it please your lordship to order someone to go and fetch the stone, I hope that it will bear witness to the truth. We will remain here, the Jew and I, until the stone arrives; I will send for it at my master Setoc's expense."

"I am quite willing that that should be done," answered the judge; and then he proceeded to dispatch other business.

At the end of the sitting he said to Zadig:

"Well, your stone is not arrived yet, is it?"

The Jew laughed, and answered:

"Your lordship would have to remain here till tomorrow before the stone could be brought; it is more than six miles away, and it would take fifteen men to move it."

"Now then," exclaimed Zadig, "did I not say well that the stone itself would bear witness? Since this man knows where it is, he acknowledges that upon it the money was counted." The Jew was abashed, and was soon obliged to confess the whole truth. The judge ordered him to be bound to the stone, without eating or drinking, until the five hundred ounces should be restored, and it was not long before they were paid.

After that, Zadig the slave was held in high esteem throughout Arabia, and so was the stone.

Chapter 11
The Funeral Pile

SETOC WAS SO enchanted with his slave that he made him his intimate friend. He could no more dispense with him than the king of Babylon had done; and Zadig was glad that Setoc had no wife. He found in his master an excellent disposition, with much integrity and good sense; but he was sorry to see that he worshiped the host of heaven (that is to say, the sun, moon, and stars), according to the ancient custom of Arabia. He spoke to him sometimes on the subject with judicious caution. At last he told him that they were material bodies like other things, which were no more worthy of his adoration than a tree or a rock.

"But," said Setoc, "they are immortal beings, from whom we derive all the benefits we enjoy; they animate nature, and regulate the seasons; besides, they are so far from us that one cannot help worshiping them."

"You receive more advantages," answered Zadig, "from the waters of the Red Sea, which bear your merchandise to India. Why may it not be as ancient as the stars? And if you adore what is far away from you, you ought to adore the land of the Gangarides, which lies at the very end of the world."

"No," said Setoc; "the stars are so bright that I cannot refrain from worshiping them."

When the evening was come, Zadig lighted a great number of candles in the tent where he was to sup with Setoc; and, as soon as his patron appeared, he threw himself on his knees before those wax lights, saying:

"Eternal and brilliant luminaries, be ever propitious to me!"

Having offered this prayer, he sat down to table without paying any attention to Setoc.

"What is that you are doing?" asked Setoc in astonishment.

"I am doing what you do," answered Zadig; "I adore these candles, and neglect their master and mine."

Setoc understood the profound meaning of this parable. The wisdom of his slave entered into his soul; he no longer lavished his incense upon created things, but worshiped the Eternal Being who had made them.

There prevailed at that time in Arabia a frightful custom, which came originally from Scythia, and which, having established itself in India through the influence of the Brahmins, threatened to invade all the East. When a married man died, and his favorite wife wished to obtain a reputation for scanctity, she used to burn herself in public on her husband's corpse. A solemn festival was held on such occasions, called "The Funeral Pile of Widowhood," and that tribe in which there had been the greatest number of women consumed in this way was held in the highest honor. An Arab of Setoc's tribe having died, his widow, named Almona, who was very devout, made known the day and hour when she would cast herself into the fire to the sound of drums and trumpets. Zadig showed Setoc how contrary to the interests of the human race this horrible custom was, for young widows were every day allowed to burn themselves who might have presented children to the State, or at least have brought up those they already had; and he made him agree that so barbarous an institution ought, if possible, to be abolished.

Setoc replied: "It is more than a thousand years since the women acquired the right of burning themselves. Which of us will dare to change a law which time has consecrated? Is there anything more venerable than an ancient abuse?"

"Reason is more ancient," rejoined Zadig. "Do you speak to the chiefs of the tribes, and I will go and find the young widow."

He obtained admission to her presence; and after having insinuated himself into her good graces by commending her beauty, and after having said what a pity it was to commit such charms to the flames, he praised her again on the score of her constancy and courage.

"You must have loved your husband wonderfully?" said he.

"I? Oh no, not at all," answered the Arab lady. "I could not bear him, he was so brutal and jealous; but I am firmly resolved to throw myself on his funeral pile."

"Apparently," said Zadig, "there must be some very delicious pleasure in being burned alive."

"Ah! It makes nature shudder to think of it," said the lady; "but I must put up with it. I am a pious person, and I should lose my reputation and be mocked by everybody if I did not burn myself."

Zadig, having brought her to admit that she was burning herself for the sake of other people and out of vanity, spoke to her for a long time in a manner calculated to make her a little in love with life, and even managed to inspire her with some kindly feeling towards himself.

"What would you do now," said he, "if you were not moved by vanity to burn yourself?"

"Alas!" said the lady, "I think that I should ask you to marry me."

Zadig was too much engrossed with thoughts of Astarte to take any notice of this declaration, but he instantly went to the chiefs of the different tribes, told them what had passed, and advised them to make a law by which no widow should be allowed to burn herself until after she had had a private interview with a young man for the space of a whole hour. Since that time no lady has burned herself in Arabia. To Zadig alone was the credit due for having abolished in one day so cruel a custom, and one that had lasted so many ages. Thus he became the benefactor of all Arabia.

Chapter 12

The Supper

SETOC, WHO COULD not part from the man in whom wisdom dwelt, brought him to the great fair of Bassora, whither the wealthiest merchants of the habitable globe were wont to resort. It was no little consolation to Zadig to see so many men of different countries assembled in the same place. It seemed to him that the universe was one large family which gathered together at Bassora. The second day after their arrival Zadig found himself at table with an Egyptian, an Indian from the banks of the Ganges, an inhabitant of China, a Greek, a Celt, and several other foreigners, who, in their frequent voyages to the Persian Gulf, had learned enough Arabic to make themselves understood. The Egyptian appeared exceedingly angry. "What an abominable country Bassora is!" said he; "I cannot get a loan here of a thousand ounces of gold on the best security in the world."

"How is that?" said Setoc; "on what security was that sum refused you?"

"On the body of my aunt," answered the Egyptian; "she was the worthiest woman in Egypt. She always accompanied me on my journeys, and died on the way hither. I have turned her into one of the finest mummies to be had, and in my own country I could get whatever I wanted by giving her in pledge. It is very strange that no one here will lend me even a thousand ounces of gold on such sound security."

In spite of his indignation, he was just on the point of devouring a capital boiled fowl, when the Indian, taking him by the hand, exclaimed in a doleful voice, "Ah! what are you about to do?"

"To eat this fowl," said the man with the mummy.

"Beware of what you are doing," said the man from the Ganges; "it may be that the soul of the departed has passed into the body of that fowl, and you would not wish to run the risk of eating up your aunt. To cook fowls is plainly an outrage upon nature."

"What do you mean with your nonsense about nature and fowls?" returned the wrathful Egyptian. "We worship an ox, and yet eat beef for all that."

"You worship an ox! Is it possible?" said the man from the Ganges.

"There is nothing more certain," replied the other; "we have done so for a hundred and thirty-five thousand years, and no one among us has any fault to find with it."

"Ah! A hundred and thirty-five thousand years!" said the Indian. "There must be a little exaggeration there; India has only been inhabited eighty thousand years, and we are undoubtedly more ancient than you are; and Brahma had forbidden us to eat oxen before you ever thought of putting them on your altars and on your spits."

"An odd kind of animal, this Brahma of yours, to be compared with Apis!" said the Egyptian. "What fine things now has your Brahma ever done?"

"It was he," the Brahmin answered, "who taught men to read and write, and to whom all the world owes the game of chess."

"You are wrong," said a Chaldean who was sitting near him; "it is to the fish Oannes that we owe such great benefits; and it is right to render our homage to him alone. Anybody will tell you that he was a divine being, that he had a golden tail and a handsome human head, and that he used to leave the water to come to preach on land for three hours every day. He had sundry children who were all kings, as everyone knows. I have his likeness at home, to which I pay all due reverence. We may eat as much beef as we please, but there is no doubt that it is a very great sin to cook fish. Moreover, you are, both of you, of too mean and too modern an origin to argue with me about anything. The Egyptian nation counts only one hundred and thirty-five thousand years, and the Indians can boast of no more than eighty thousand, while we have almanacs that go back four thousand centuries. Believe me, renounce your follies, and I will give each of you a beautiful likeness of Oannes."

The Chinaman here put in his word, and said:

"I have a strong respect for the Egyptians, the Chaldeans, the Greeks, the Celts, Brahma, the ox Apis, and the fine fish Oannes, but it may be that Li or Tien,[7] by whichever name one may choose to call him, is well worth any number of oxen and fishes. I will say nothing about my country; it is as large as the lands of Egypt, Chaldea, and India all put together. I will enter into no dispute touching antiquity, because it is enough to be happy, and it is a very little matter to be ancient. But if there were any need to speak about almanacs, I could tell you that all Asia consults ours, and that we had very good ones before anything at all was known of arithmetic in Chaldea."

"You are a set of ignoramuses, all of you!" cried the Greek; "is it possible that you do not know that Chaos is the father of all things, and that form and matter have brought the world into the state in which it is?"

This Greek spoke for a long time, but he was at last interrupted by the Celt, who, having drunk deeply while the others were disputing, now thought himself wiser than any of them, and affirmed with an oath that there was nothing worth the trouble of talking about except Teutates and the mistletoe that grows on an oak; that, as for himself, he always had some mistletoe in his pocket; that the Scythians, his forefathers, were the only honest people that had ever been in the world; that they had indeed sometimes eaten men, but that no one ought to be prevented by that from having a profound respect for his nation; and finally, that if anyone spoke evil of Teutates, he would teach him how to behave.

Thereupon the quarrel waxed hot, and Setoc saw that in another moment there would be bloodshed at the table, when Zadig, who had kept silent during the whole dispute, at last rose. He addressed himself first to the Celt as the most violent of them all; he told him that he was in the right, and asked him for a piece of mistletoe. He commended the Greek for his eloquence, and soothed the general irritation. He said very little to the Chinaman, because he had been the most reasonable of them all. Then he said to the whole party:

"My friends, you were going to quarrel for nothing, for you are all of the same opinion."

When they heard him say that, they all loudly protested.

"Is it not true," he said to the Celt, "that you do not worship this mistletoe, but Him who made the mistletoe and the oak?"

"Assuredly," answered the Celt.

"And you, my Egyptian friend, revere, as it would seem, in a certain ox Him who has given you oxen, is it not so?"

"Yes," said the Egyptian.

"The fish Oannes," continued Zadig, "must give place to Him who made the sea and the fishes."

"Granted," said the Chaldean.

"The Indian," added Zadig, "and the Chinaman recognize, like you, a first principle; I did not understand very well the admirable remarks made by the Greek, but I am sure that he also admits the existence of a Supreme Being, upon whom form and matter depend."

The Greek who was so much admired said that Zadig had seized his meaning very well.

"You are all then of the same opinion," replied Zadig, "and there is nothing left to quarrel over;" at which all the company embraced him.

Setoc, after having sold his merchandise at a high price, brought his friend Zadig back with him to his tribe. On their arrival Zadig learned that he had been tried in his absence, and that he was going to be burned at a slow fire.

Chapter 13

The Assignation

DURING HIS JOURNEY to Bassora, the priests of the stars had determined to punish Zadig. The precious stones and ornaments of the young widows whom they sent to the funeral pile were their acknowledged perquisite; it was in truth the least they could do to burn Zadig for the ill turn he had done them. Accordingly they accused him of holding erroneous views about the host of heaven; they gave testimony against him on oath that they had heard him say that the stars did not set in the sea. This frightful blasphemy made the judges shudder; they were ready to rend their garments when they heard those impious words, and they would have done so, without a doubt, if Zadig had had the means wherewith to pay them compensation, but dreadfully shocked as they were, they contented themselves with condemning him to be burned at a slow fire.

Setoc, in despair, exerted his influence in vain to save his friend; he was soon obliged to hold his peace. The young widow Almona, who had acquired a strong appetite for life, thanks to Zadig, resolved to rescue him from the stake, the misuse of which he had taught her to recognize. She turned her scheme over and over in her head, without speaking of it to anyone. Zadig was to be executed the next day, and she had only that night to save him in. This is how she set about the business, like a charitable and discreet woman. She anointed herself with perfumes; she enhanced her charms by the richest and most seductive attire, and went to ask the chief priest of the stars for a private audience. When she was ushered into the presence of that venerable old man, she addressed him in these terms:

"Eldest son of the Great Bear, brother of the Bull, and cousin of the Great Dog" (such were the pontiff's titles), "I come to confide to you my scruples. I greatly fear that I have committed an enormous sin in not burning myself on my dear husband's funeral pyre. In truth, what had I worth preserving? A body liable to decay, and which is already quite withered." Saying these words, she drew up her long silk sleeves, and displayed her bare arms, of admirable form and dazzling whiteness. "You see," said she, "how little it is worth."

The pontiff thought in his heart that it was worth a great deal. His eyes said so, and his mouth confirmed it; he swore that he had never in his life seen such beautiful arms.

"Alas!" said the widow, "my arms may be a little less deformed than the rest; but you will admit that my neck was unworthy of any consideration," and she let him see the most charming bosom that nature had ever formed. A rosebud on an apple of ivory would have appeared beside it nothing better than madder upon box-wood, and lambs just come up from the washing would have seemed brown and sallow. This neck; her large black eyes, in which a tender fire glowed softly with languishing luster; her cheeks, enlivened with the loveliest crimson mingled with the whiteness of the purest milk; her nose, which was not at all like the tower of Mount Lebanon; her lips, which were like two settings of coral enclosing the most beautiful pearls in the Arabian sea; all these charms conspired to make the old man fancy himself a youth of twenty summers. With stammering tongue he made a tender declaration; and Almona, seeing how he was smitten, craved pardon for Zadig.

"Alas!" said he, "my lovely lady, though I might grant you his pardon, my indulgence would be of no use, as the order would have to be signed by three others of my colleagues."

"Sign it all the same," said Almona.

"Willingly," said the priest, "on condition that your favors shall be the price of my compliance."

"You do me too much honor," said Almona; "only be pleased to come to my chamber after sunset; when the bright star *Sheat* shall rise above the horizon; you will find me on a rose-colored sofa, and you shall deal with your servant as you may be able."

Then she went away, carrying with her the signature, and left the old man full of amorous passion and of diffidence as to his powers. He employed the rest of the day in bathing; he drank a liquid compounded of the cinnamon of Ceylon, and the precious spices of Tidor and Ternat, and waited with impatience for the star *Sheat* to appear.

Meanwhile the fair Almona went in search of the second pontiff, who assured her that the sun, the moon, and all the lights of heaven were nothing but faint marsh fires in comparison with her charms. She asked of him the same favor, and he offered to grant it on the same terms. She allowed her scruples to be overcome, and made an appointment with the second pontiff for the rising of the star *Algenib*. Thence she proceeded to the houses of the third and fourth priests, getting from each his signature, and making one star after another the signal for a secret assignation. Then she sent letters to the judges, requesting them to come and see her on a matter of importance. When they appeared, she showed them the four names, and told them at what price the priests had sold Zadig's pardon. Each of the latter arrived at his appointed hour, and was greatly astonished to find his colleagues there, and still more at seeing the judges, before whom they were exposed to open shame. Thus Zadig was saved, and Setoc was so delighted with Almona's cleverness, that he made her his wife.

Chapter 14

The Dance

SETOC WAS ENGAGED to go on matters of business to the island of Serendib,[8] but the first month of marriage, which is, as everyone knows, the moon of honey, permitted him neither to quit his wife, nor even to imagine that he could ever quit her; so he requested his friend Zadig to make the voyage on his behalf.

"Alas!" said Zadig, "must I put a yet wider distance between the beautiful Astarte and myself? But I must oblige my benefactors." He spoke, he wept, and he set forth on his journey.

He was not long in the island of Serendib before he began to be regarded as an extraordinary man. He became umpire in all disputes between the merchants, the friend of the wise, and the trusted counselor of that small number of persons who are willing to take advice. The king wished to see and hear him. He soon recognized all Zadig's worth, placed reliance on his wisdom, and made him his friend. The king's intimacy and esteem made Zadig tremble. Night and day he was pierced with anguish at the misfortune which Moabdar's kindness had brought upon him.

"The king is pleased with me," said he; "how shall I escape ruin?"

He could not however decline his majesty's attentions; for it must be confessed that Nabussan, King of Serendib, the son of Nussanab, the son of Nabassan, the son of Sanbusna, was one of the best princes in Asia; when anyone spoke to him, it was difficult not to love him.

This good monarch was continually praised, deceived, and robbed; officials vied with each other in plundering his treasury. The receiver-general of the island of Serendib always set the example, and was faithfully followed by the others. The king knew it, and had time after time changed his treasurer; but he had not been able to change the time-honored fashion of dividing the royal revenue into two unequal parts, the smaller of which always fell to His Majesty, and the larger to the administrative staff.

King Nabussan confided his difficulty to the wise Zadig: "You who know so many fine things," said he, "can you think of no method of enabling me to find a treasurer who will not rob me?"

"Assuredly," answered Zadig; "I know an infallible way of giving you a man who has clean hands."

The king was charmed, and, embracing him, asked how he was to proceed.

"All you will have to do," said Zadig, "is to cause all who shall present themselves for the dignity of treasurer to dance, and he who dances most lightly will be infallibly the most honest man."

"You are joking," said the king; "truly a droll way of choosing a receiver of my revenues! What! Do you mean to say that the one who cuts the highest capers will prove the most honest and capable financier?"

"I will not answer for his capability," returned Zadig; "but I assure you that he will undoubtedly be the most honest."

Zadig spoke with so much confidence that the king thought he had some supernatural secret for recognizing financiers.

"I am not fond of the supernatural," said Zadig; "people and books that deal in prodigies have always been distasteful to me; if Your Majesty will allow me to make the trial I propose, you will be well enough convinced that my secret is the easiest and most simple thing in the world."

Nabussan, King of Serendib, was far more astonished at hearing that this secret was a simple matter, than if it had been presented to him as a miracle.

"Well then," said the king, "do as you shall think proper."

"Give me a free hand," said Zadig, "and you will gain by this experiment more than you think."

The same day he issued a public notice that all who aspired to the post of receiver-in-chief of the revenues of His Gracious Majesty Nabussan, son of Nussanab, were to present themselves in garments of light silk, on the first day of the month of the Crocodile, in the king's antechamber. They duly put in an appearance to the number of sixty-four. Fiddlers were posted in an adjoining hall; all was ready for dancing; but the door of the hall was fastened, and it was necessary, in order to enter it, to pass along a little gallery which was pretty dark. An usher was sent to conduct each candidate, one after another, along this passage, in which he was left alone for a few minutes. The king, prompted by Zadig, had spread out all his treasures in this gallery. When all the competitors had reached the hall, his majesty gave orders that they should begin to dance. Never did men dance more heavily and with less grace; they all kept their heads down, their backs bent, and their hands glued to their sides.

"What rogues!" said Zadig, under his breath.

There was only one among them who stepped out freely, with head erect, a steady eye, and outstretched arms, body straight, and legs firm.

"Ah! The honest fellow! The worthy man!" said Zadig.

The king embraced this good dancer, and declared him treasurer; whereas all the others were punished with a fine, and that most justly, for each one of them, during the time that he was in the gallery, had filled his pockets so that he could hardly walk. The king was grieved for the honor of human nature that out of those sixty-four dancers there should have been sixty-three thieves. The dark gallery was henceforth called *The Corridor of Temptation*. In Persia those sixty-three gentlemen would have been impaled; in other countries a court of justice would have been held which would have consumed in legal expenses three times as much as had been stolen; while in yet another kingdom they would have procured a complete acquittal for themselves, and brought the nimble dancer to disgrace; at Serendib they were only condemned to increase the public funds, for Nabussan was very indulgent.

He was also very grateful; he gave to Zadig a sum of money greater than any treasurer had stolen from his master the king. Zadig availed himself of it to send expresses to Babylon, who were to bring him information of Astarte's fate. His voice trembled while giving this order, his blood flowed back towards his heart, a mist covered his eyes, and his soul was ready to take its flight. The messenger departed: Zadig saw him embark. He returned to the king, seeing no one, fancying himself in his own chamber, and pronouncing the name of "love."

"Ah! love," said the king; "that is precisely what is the matter with me; you have rightly divined where my trouble lies. What a great man you are! I hope you will teach me how to recognize a faithful and devoted wife, as you have enabled me to find a disinterested treasurer."

Zadig, having recovered his wits, promised to serve him in love as well as in finance, although the undertaking seemed still more difficult.

Chapter 15

Blue Eyes

"My body and my heart—," said the king to Zadig.

At these words the Babylonian could not refrain from interrupting His Majesty.

"How glad I am," said he, "that you did not say *my heart and soul*! For one hears nothing else but those words in every conversation at Babylon, and one sees nothing but books devoted to discussions on the heart and soul, written by people who have neither one nor the other. But please, sire, proceed."

Nabussan then continued:

"My body and my heart are predisposed by destiny to love; the former of these two powers has every reason to be satisfied. I have here a hundred women at my disposal, all beautiful, buxom, and obliging, even voluptuously inclined, or pretending to be so when with me. My heart is not nearly so well off. I have found only too often that they lavish all their caresses on the King of Serendib, and care very little for Nabussan. It is not that I think my women unfaithful; but I would fain find a soul to be my own; I would resign for such a treasure the hundred beauties of whose charms I am master. See if, out of these hundred ladies of my harem, you can find me a single one by whom I may feel sure that I am loved?"

Zadig answered him as he had done on the subject of the financiers:—

"Sire, leave the matter to me; but allow me first to dispose of what you displayed in 'The Corridor of Temptation.' I will render you a good account of all, and you shall lose nothing by it."

The king gave him unfettered discretion. He chose in Serendib thirty-three little hunchbacks, the ugliest he could find, thirty-three of the most handsome pages, and thirty-three of the most eloquent and most robust bonzes. He left them all at liberty to enter the ladies' private chambers. Each little hunchback had four thousand gold pieces to give them, and the very first day all the hunchbacks were happy. The pages, who had nothing to give away but themselves, failed to achieve a triumph till the end of two or three days. The bonzes had a little more difficulty; but at last thirty-three fair devotees surrendered to them. The king, through the shutter-blinds which admitted a view into each chamber, witnessed all these experiments, and was not a little astonished. Of his hundred women, ninety-nine had succumbed before his eyes. There yet remained one who was quite young and freshly imported, whom His Majesty had never admitted to his arms. One, two, three hunchbacks were successively told off to make her offers which rose to the sum of twenty thousand pieces; she was incorruptible, and could not help laughing at the idea which had entered into these hunchbacks' heads that money could render them less deformed. The two handsomest of the pages were presented to her; she said that she thought the king still more handsome. The most eloquent and afterwards the most intrepid of the bonzes were let loose upon her; she found the first an idle babbler, and would not deign even to form an opinion on the merits of the second.

"The heart is everything," said she; "I will never yield either to the gold of a hunchback, or the personal attractions of a young man, or the cunning enticements of a bonze. I will love no one but Nabussan, son of Nussanab, and will wait till he condescends to love me."

The king was transported with joy, astonishment, and tenderness. He took back all the money that had won the hunchbacks their success, and made a present of it to the fair Falide (for such was the young lady's name). He gave her his heart, and she well deserved it. Never was the flower of youth so brilliant, never were the charms of beauty so enchanting. Historical veracity will not allow me to conceal the fact that she curtsied awkwardly, but she danced like a fairy, sang like a siren, and spoke like one of the graces; she was full of accomplishments and virtues.

Nabussan, loved as he was by her, adored her in his turn. But she had blue eyes, and this was the source of the greatest misfortunes. There was an ancient law which forbade the kings to love one of those women whom the Greeks in later days called βοωπις.[9] The chief of the bonzes had established this law more than five thousand years before that time, with a view to appropriating the mistress of the first king of the island of Serendib, whom the chief bonze had induced to pass an anathema upon blue eyes as a fundamental article of the constitution. All orders of society came to remonstrate with Nabussan. They publicly declared that the last days of the kingdom had arrived, that iniquity had reached its height, and that all nature was threatened with some untoward accident; that, in a word, Nabussan, son of Nussanab, was in love with two big blue eyes. The hunchbacks, financiers, bonzes, and brunettes, filled the palace with complaints.

The wild tribes that inhabit the north of Serendib took advantage of the general discontent to make an incursion into the territory of the good Nabussan. He demanded subsidies from his subjects; the bonzes, who owned half the revenues of the state, contented themselves with raising their hands to heaven, and refused to put them into their coffers to help the king. They offered up grand prayers to fine music, and left the State a prey to the barbarians.

"O my dear Zadig! Will you rescue me again from this horrible embarrassment?" dolefully exclaimed Nabussan.

"Very willingly," answered Zadig. "You shall have as much money from the bonzes as you wish. Abandon to the enemy the lands on which their mansions are built, and only defend your own."

Nabussan did not fail to follow this advice. The bonzes thereupon came and threw themselves at the king's feet, imploring his assistance. The king answered them in beautiful strains of music, the words to which they were an accompaniment being prayers to Heaven for the preservation of their lands. The bonzes at last gave some money, and the king brought the war to a prosperous conclusion. Thus Zadig, by his wise and successful counsel, and by his important services, drew upon himself the irreconcilable hatred of the most powerful men in the State: the bonzes and the brunettes took an oath to ruin him; the financiers and the hunchbacks did not spare him, but did all they could to make him suspected by the excellent Nabussan. "Good offices remain in the antechamber when suspicions enter the closet," as Zoroaster has wisely observed. Every day there were fresh accusations; if the first was repelled, the second might graze the skin, the third wound, and the fourth be fatal.

Zadig, after having advantageously transacted the business of his friend Setoc and sent him his money, thought of nothing now in his alarm but of leaving the island, and resolved to go himself in search of tidings of Astarte.

"For," said he, "if I stay in Serendib, the bonzes will cause me to be impaled. . . . But where can I go? In Egypt I shall be a slave; burnt, in all likelihood, in Arabia; strangled at Babylon. Still I must know what has become of Astarte. . . . Let us be gone, and see for what my sad destiny reserves me."

Chapter 16

The Brigand

ON ARRIVING AT the frontier which separates Arabia Petræa from Syria, as he was passing near a strong castle, a party of armed Arabs sallied forth. He saw himself surrounded, and the men cried out: "All that you have belongs to us, and your body belongs to our master."

Zadig, by way of answer, drew his sword; his servant, who had plenty of courage, did the same. They routed and slew the Arabs who first laid hands on them; their assailants now numbered twice as many as before, but they were not daunted, and resolved to die fighting. Then were seen two men defending themselves against a multitude. Such a conflict could not last long. The master of the castle, whose name was Arbogad, having seen from a window the prodigies of valor performed by Zadig, conceived such an admiration for him that he hastily descended, and came in person to disperse his men and deliver the two travelers.

"All that passes over my lands is my property," said he, "as well as whatever I find on the lands of other people; but you seem to me such a brave man, that I except you from the general rule."

He made Zadig enter his castle, and bade his people treat him well. In the evening Arbogad desired Zadig to sup with him.

Now the lord of the castle was one of those Arabs who are known as *robbers*; but he sometimes did a good action among a multitude of bad ones. He robbed with fierce rapacity, and gave away freely; he was intrepid in battle, though gentle enough in society; intemperate at table, merry in his cups, and above all, full of frankness. Zadig pleased him greatly, and his animated conversation prolonged the repast. At length Arbogad said to him:

"I advise you to enroll yourself under me; you cannot do better; this calling of mine is not a bad one, and you may one day become what I now am."

"May I ask you," said Zadig, "how long you have practiced this noble profession?"

"From my tenderest youth," replied the lord of the castle. "I was the servant of an Arab who was a pretty sharp fellow; I felt my position intolerable; it drove me to despair to see that in all the earth, which belongs equally to all mankind, fortune had reserved no portion for me. I confided my trouble to an old Arab, who said to me: 'My son, do not despair; there was once upon a time a grain of sand which bewailed its fate in being a mere unheeded atom in the desert; but at the end of a few years it became a diamond, and it is now the most beautiful ornament in the King of India's crown.' This story made a great impression on me. I was the grain of sand, and I determined to become a diamond. I began by stealing two horses; I then formed a gang, and put myself in a position to rob small caravans. Thus by degrees I abolished the disproportion which existed at first between myself and other men; I had my share in the good things of this world, and was even recompensed with usury. I was held in high esteem, became a brigand chief, and obtained this castle by violence. The satrap of Syria wished to dispossess me, but I was already too rich to have anything to dread; I gave some money to the satrap, and by this means retained the castle and increased my domains. He even named me treasurer of the tribute which Arabia Petræa paid to the king of kings. I fulfilled my duty well, so far as receiving went, but utterly ignored that of payment. The Grand Desterham of Babylon sent hither in the name of King Moabdar a petty satrap, intending to have me strangled. This man arrived with his orders; I was informed of all, and caused to be strangled in his presence the four persons he had brought with him to apply the bowstring to my neck; after which I asked him what his commission to strangle me might be worth to him. He answered me that his fees might amount to three hundred pieces of gold. I made it clear to him that there was more to be gained with me. I gave him a subordinate post among my brigands, and now he is one of my smartest and wealthiest officers. Take my word for it, you will succeed as well as he. Never has there been a better season for pillage, since Moabdar is slain and all is in confusion at Babylon."

"Moabdar slain!" said Zadig; "and what has become of Queen Astarte?"

"I know nothing about her," replied Arbogad; "all I know is that Moabdar became mad and was killed, that Babylon is one vast slaughter-house, that all the empire is laid waste, that there are fine blows to be struck yet, and that I myself have done wonders in that way."

"But the queen?" said Zadig; "pray tell me, know you nothing of the fate of the queen?"

"I heard something about a prince of Hyrcania," replied he; "She is probably among his concubines, if she has not been killed in the insurrection. But I have more curiosity in the matter of plunder than of news. I have taken a good many women in my raids, but I keep none of them; I sell them at a high price if they are handsome, without inquiring who or what they are, for my customers pay nothing for rank; a queen who was ugly would find no purchaser. Maybe I have sold Queen Astarte, maybe she is dead; it matters very little to me, and I do not think you need be more concerned about her than I am."

As he spoke thus he went on drinking lustily, and mixed up all his ideas so confusedly that Zadig could extract no information out of him.

He remained confounded, overwhelmed, unable to stir. Arbogad continued to drink, told stories, constantly repeated that he was the happiest of all men, and exhorted Zadig to render himself as happy as he was. At last, becoming more and more drowsy with the fumes of wine, he gradually fell into a tranquil slumber. Zadig passed the night in a state of the most violent agitation.

"What!" said he, "The king become mad! The king killed! I cannot help lamenting him! The empire is dismembered, and this brigand is happy! Alas for fate and fortune! A robber is happy, and the most amiable object that nature ever created has perhaps perished in a frightful manner, or is living in a condition worse than death. O Astarte! what has become of you?"

At break of day he questioned all whom he met in the castle, but everybody was busy, and no one answered him: new conquests had been made during the night, and they were dividing the spoils. All that he could obtain in the confusion that prevailed was permission to depart, of which he availed himself without delay, plunged deeper than ever in painful thoughts.

Zadig walked on restless and agitated, his mind engrossed with the hapless Astarte, with the king of Babylon, with his faithful Cador, with the happy brigand Arbogad, and that capricious woman whom the Babylonians had carried off on the confines of Egypt, in short, with all the disappointments and misfortunes that he had experienced.

Chapter 17

The Fisherman

AT A DISTANCE of several leagues from Arbogad's castle, he found himself on the brink of a little river, still deploring his destiny, and regarding himself as the very personification of misery. There he saw a fisherman lying on the bank, hardly holding in his feeble hand the net which he seemed ready to drop, and lifting his eyes towards heaven.

"I am certainly the most wretched of all men," said the fisherman. "I was, as everybody allowed, the most famous seller of cream cheeses in Babylon, and I have been ruined. I had the prettiest wife that a man could possess, and she has betrayed me. A mean house was all that was left me, and I have seen it plundered and destroyed. Having taken refuge in a hut, I have no resource but fishing, and I cannot catch a single fish. O my net! I will cast you no more into the water, it is myself that I must cast therein."

Saying these words, he rose and advanced in the attitude of a man about to throw himself headlong and put an end to his life.

"What is this?" said Zadig to himself; "there are men then as miserable as I!"

Eagerness to save the fisherman's life rose as promptly as this reflection. He ran towards him, stopped, and questioned him with an air of concern and encouragement. It is said that we are less miserable when we are not alone in our misery. According to Zoroaster this is due, not to malice, but to necessity; we then feel ourselves drawn towards a victim of misfortune as a fellow sufferer. The joy of a prosperous man would seem to us an insult, but two wretched men are like two weak trees, which, leaning together, mutually strengthen each other against the tempest.

"Why do you give way to your misfortunes?" said Zadig to the fisherman.

"Because," answered he, "I see no way out of them. I was held in the highest esteem in the village of Derlback, near Babylon, and I made, with my wife's help, the best cream cheeses in the empire. Queen Astarte and the famous minister Zadig were passionately fond of them. I had supplied their houses with six hundred cheeses, and went one day into town to be paid, when, on my arrival at Babylon, I learned that the queen and Zadig had disappeared. I hastened to the house of the lord Zadig, whom I had never seen; there I found the police officers of the Grand Desterham, who, furnished with a royal warrant, were sacking his house in a perfectly straightforward and orderly manner. I flew to the queen's kitchens: some of the lords of the dresser told me that she was dead; other said that she was in prison; while others again declared that she had taken flight; but all assured me that I should be paid nothing for my cheeses. I went with my wife to the house of the lord Orcan, who was one of my customers, and we asked him to protect us in our distress. He granted his protection to my wife, and refused it to me. She was whiter than those cream cheeses with which my troubles began, and the gleam of Tyrian purple was not more brilliant than the carnation which animated that whiteness. It was this which made the lord Orcan keep her and drive me away from his house. I wrote to my dear wife the letter of a desperate man. She said to the messenger who brought it:

"'Oh! Ah, yes! I know something of the man who writes me this letter. I have heard people speak of him; they say he makes capital cream cheeses. Let him send me some, and see that he is paid for them.'"

"In my unhappy state I determined to have recourse to justice. I had six ounces of gold left; I had to give two ounces to the lawyer whom I consulted, two to the attorney who undertook my case, and two to the secretary of the first judge. When all this was done, my suit was not yet commenced, and I had already spent more money than my cheeses and my wife were worth. I returned to my village, with the intention of selling my house in order to recover my wife.

"My house was well worth sixty ounces of gold, but people saw that I was poor and forced to sell. The first man to whom I applied offered me thirty ounces for it, the second twenty, and the third ten. I was ready at last to take anything, so blinded was I, when a prince of Hyrcania came to Babylon, and ravaged all the country on his way. My house was first sacked and then burned.

"Having thus lost my money, my wife, and my house, I retired to this part of the country where you see me. I tried to support myself by fishing, but the fishes mock me as much as men do; I take nothing, I am dying of hunger, and had it not been for you, my illustrious consoler, I should have perished in the river."

The fisherman did not tell his story all at once; for every moment Zadig in his agitation would break in with: "What! Do you know nothing of what has befallen the queen?" "No, my lord," the fisherman would make reply; "but I know that the queen and Zadig have not paid me for my cream cheeses, that my wife has been taken from me, and that I am in despair."

"I feel confident," said Zadig, "that you will not lose all your money. I have heard people speak of this Zadig; he is an honest man, and if he returns to Babylon, as he hopes to do, he will give you more than he owes you. But as to your wife, who is not so honest, I recommend you not to try to recover her. Take my advice, go to Babylon; I shall be there before you, because I am on horseback, and you are on foot. Apply to the most noble Cador, tell him you have met his friend, and wait for me at his house. Go; perhaps you will not always be unhappy."

"O mighty Ormuzd," continued he, "thou dost make use of me to console this man, of whom wilt thou make use to console me?"

So saying, he gave the fisherman half of all the money he had brought from Arabia, and the fisherman, astonished and delighted, kissed the feet of Cador's friend, and said: "You are an angel sent to save me."

Meanwhile Zadig continued to ask for news, shedding tears as he did so.

"What, my lord," cried the fisherman, "can you then be unhappy, you who bestow bounty?"

"A hundred times more unhappy than you," answered Zadig.

"But how can it be," said the simple fellow, "that he who gives is more to be pitied than he who receives?"

"Because," replied Zadig, "your greatest misfortune was a hungry belly, and because my misery has its seat in the heart."

"Has Orcan taken away your wife?" said the fisherman.

This question recalled all his adventures to Zadig's mind; he repeated the catalogue of his misfortunes, beginning with the queen's bitch, up to the time of his arrival at the castle of the brigand Arbogad.

"Ah!" said he to the fisherman, "Orcan deserves to be punished. But it is generally such people as he who are the favorites of fortune. Be that as it may, go to the house of the lord Cador, and wait for me."

They parted. The fisherman walked on thanking his stars, and Zadig pressed forward still accusing his own.

Chapter 18
The Cockatrice

HAVING ARRIVED AT a beautiful meadow, Zadig saw there several women searching for something with great diligence. He took the liberty of approaching one of them, and of asking her if he might have the honor of helping them in their search.

"Take good heed not to do that," answered the Syrian damsel; "what we are looking for can only be touched with impunity by women."

"That is very strange," said Zadig; "may I venture to ask you to tell me what it is that only women are allowed to touch?"

"A cockatrice," said she.

"A cockatrice, madam! And for what reason, if you please, are you looking for a cockatrice?"

"It is for our lord and master, Ogul, whose castle you see on the bank of that river, at the end of the meadow. We are his most humble slaves; the lord Ogul is ill, his physician has ordered him to eat a cockatrice stewed in rose-water, and, as it is a very rare animal, and never allows itself to be taken except by women, the lord Ogul has promised to choose for his well-beloved wife, whichever of us shall bring him a cockatrice. Let me pursue the search, if you please; for you see what it would cost me, if I were anticipated by my companions."

Zadig left this Syrian girl and the others to look for their cockatrice, and continued to walk through the meadow. When he reached the brink of a little stream, he found there another lady lying on the turf, but not in search of anything. Her figure appeared majestic, but her countenance was covered with a veil. She was leaning over the stream; deep sighs escaped from her mouth. She held in her hand a little rod, with which she was tracing characters on the fine sand which lay between the grass and the stream. Zadig had the curiosity to look and see what this woman was writing. He drew near, and saw the letter Z, then an A. He was astonished. When there appeared a D, he started. Never was there surprise to equal his, when he saw the two last letters of his name. He remained some time without moving, then, breaking the silence, he exclaimed in an agitated voice:

"O noble lady, pardon a stranger who is in distress if he ventures to ask you by what astonishing chance I find here the name of Zadig traced by your adorable hand."

At that voice, at those words, the lady raised her veil with a trembling hand, turned her eyes on Zadig, uttered a cry of tenderness, surprise, and joy, and, overcome by all the varied emotions which simultaneously assailed her soul, she fell fainting into his arms. It was Astarte herself, it was the queen of Babylon, it was she whom Zadig adored, and whom he reproached himself for adoring, it was she for whom he had wept so much, and for whom he had so often dreaded the worst stroke of fate. For a moment he was deprived of the use of his senses, then, fixing his gaze on Astarte's eyes, which languidly opened once more with an expression in which confusion was mingled with tenderness, he cried:

"O immortal powers, who preside over the destinies of feeble mortals! Do ye indeed restore Astarte to me? At what a time, in what a place, and in what a condition do I see her again!"

He threw himself on his knees before Astarte and applied his forehead to the dust of her feet. The queen of Babylon lifted him up, and made him sit beside her on the bank of the stream, while she repeatedly dried her eyes from which tears would soon begin again to flow. Twenty times at least did she take up the thread of the discourse which her sighs interrupted; she questioned him as to what strange chance brought them once more together, and she anticipated his answers by suddenly asking fresh questions. She began to relate her own misfortunes, and then wished to know those of Zadig. At last, both of them having somewhat appeased the tumult of their souls, Zadig told her in a few words how it came to pass that he found himself in that meadow.

"But, O unhappy and honored queen, how is it that I find you in this remote spot, clad as a slave, and accompanied by other women slaves who are searching for a cockatrice to be stewed in rose-water by a physician's order?"

"While they are looking for their cockatrice," said the fair Astarte, "I will inform you of all that I have suffered, and of how much I have ceased to blame heaven now that I see you again. You know that the king, my husband, took it ill that you were the most amiable of all men, and it was for this reason that he one night took the resolution to have you strangled and me poisoned. You know how heaven permitted my little mute to give me warning of His Sublime Majesty's orders. Hardly had the faithful Cador forced you to obey me and to go away, when he ventured to enter my chamber in the middle of the night by a secret passage. He carried me off, and brought me to the temple of Ormuzd, where his brother, the magian, shut me up in a gigantic statue, the base of which touches the foundations of the temple while its head reaches to the roof. I was as buried there, but waited on by the magian and in want of none of the necessaries of life. Meanwhile at daybreak His Majesty's apothecary entered my chamber with a draught compounded of henbane, opium, black hellebore, and aconite; and another official went to your apartment with a bowstring of blue silk. Both places were found empty. Cador, the better to deceive him, went to the king, and pretended to accuse us both. He said that you had taken the road to India, and that I had gone towards Memphis; so officers were sent after each of us.

"The messengers who went in search of me did not know me by sight, for I had hardly ever shown my face to any man but yourself, and that in my husband's presence and by his command. They hastened off in pursuit of me, guided by the description that had been given them of my person. A woman of much the same height as myself, and who had, it may be, superior charms, presented herself to their eyes on the borders of Egypt. She was evidently a fugitive and in distress; they had no doubt that this woman was the queen of Babylon, and they brought her to Moabdar. Their mistake at first threw the king into a violent rage; but ere long, taking a nearer look at the woman, he perceived that she was very beautiful, which gave him some consolation. She was called Missouf. I have been told since that the name signifies in the Egyptian tongue *the capricious beauty*. Such in truth she was, but she had as much artfulness as caprice. She pleased Moabdar and brought him into subjection to such a degree that she made him declare her his wife. Thereupon her character developed itself in all its extravagance; she fearlessly gave herself up to every foolish freak of her imagination. She wished to compel the chief of the magi, who was old and gouty, to dance before her; and when he refused she persecuted him most bitterly. She ordered her master of the house to make her a jam tart. In vain did the master of the house represent to her that he was not a pastry cook: he must make the tart; and he was driven from office because it was too much burned. She gave the post of master of horse to her dwarf, and the place of chancellor to a page. It was thus that she governed Babylon, while all regretted that they had lost me. The king, who had been a tolerably just and reasonable man until the moment when he had determined to poison me and to have you strangled, seemed now to have drowned his virtues in the exorbitant love that he had for the capricious beauty. He came to the temple on the great day of the sacred fire, and I saw him implore the gods on behalf of Missouf, at the feet of the image in which I was confined. I lifted up my voice, and cried aloud to him:

" 'The gods reject the prayers of a king who is become a tyrant, who has been minded to put to death a sensible wife to marry a woman of the most extravagant whims.'

"Moabdar was so confounded at these words, that his head became disordered. The oracle that I had delivered, and Missouf's domineering temper, sufficed to deprive him of his senses, and in a few days he became quite mad.

"His madness, which seemed a punishment from heaven, was the signal for revolt. There was a general insurrection, and all men ran to take up arms. Babylon, so long plunged in effeminate idleness, became the scene of a frightful civil war. I was drawn forth from the cavity of my statue, and placed at the head of one party. Cador hastened to Memphis, to bring you back to Babylon. The prince of Hyrcania, hearing of these fatal dissensions, came back with his army to form a third party in Chaldea. He attacked the king, who fled before him with his wayward Egyptian. Moabdar died pierced with wounds, and Missouf fell into the hands of the conqueror. It was my misfortune to be myself taken prisoner by a party of Hyrcanians, and I was brought before the prince at precisely the same time as they were bringing in Missouf. You will be pleased, no doubt, to hear that the prince thought me more beautiful than the Egyptian; but you will be sorry to learn that he destined me for his harem. He told me very decidedly that as soon as he should have finished a military expedition which he was about to undertake, he would come and keep me company. You may fancy my distress! The tie that bound me to Moabdar was broken, and I might have been Zadig's, if this barbarian had not cast his chains round me. I answered him with all the pride that my rank and my resentment gave me. I had always heard it said that heaven has connected with persons of my condition a greatness of character, which, with a word or a look, can reduce the presumptuous to an humble sense of that deep respect which they have dared to disregard. I spoke like a queen, but found myself treated like a domestic. The Hyrcanian, without deigning to address to me even a single word, told his black eunuch that I was a saucy minx, but that he thought me pretty; so he bade him take care of me, and subject me to the diet of his favorites, that I might recover my complexion, and be rendered more worthy of his favors by the time when he might find it convenient to honor me with them. I told him that I would sooner kill myself. He answered, laughing, that there was no fear of that, and that he was used to such displays of affectation; whereupon he left me like a man who has just put a parrot into his aviary. What a state of things for the first queen in all the world—I will say more, for a heart which was devoted to Zadig!"

At these words Zadig threw himself at her knees, and bathed them with tears. Astarte raised him tenderly, and continued thus:

"I saw myself in the power of a barbarian, and a rival of the crazy woman who was my fellow prisoner. She told me what had befallen her in Egypt. I conjectured from the description she gave of your person, from the time of the occurrence, from the dromedary on which you were mounted, and from all the circumstances of the case, that it was Zadig who had fought in her behalf. I had no doubt that you were at Memphis, and resolved to betake myself thither.

" 'Beautiful Missouf,' said I, 'you are much more pleasing than I am, and will entertain the prince of Hyrcania far better than I can do. Help me to effect my escape; you will then reign alone, and render me happy in ridding yourself of a rival.'

"Missouf arranged with me the means of my flight, and I departed secretly with an Egyptian woman slave.

"I had nearly reached Arabia, when a notorious robber, named Arbogad, carried me off, and sold me to some merchants, who brought me to this castle where the lord Ogul resides. He bought me without knowing who I was. He is a man of pleasure whose only object in life is good cheer, and who is convinced that God has sent him into the world to sit at table. He is excessively fat, and is constantly on the point of suffocation. His physician, in whom he believes little enough when his digestion is all right, exerts a despotic sway over him whenever he has eaten too much. He has persuaded him that he can cure him with a cockatrice stewed in rose-water. The lord Ogul has promised his hand to whichever of his female slaves shall bring him a cockatrice. You see how I leave them to vie with one another in their eagerness to win this honor, for, since heaven has permitted me to see you again, I have less desire than ever to find his cockatrice."

Then Astarte and Zadig gave expression to all that tender feelings had long repressed,—all that their love and misfortunes could inspire in hearts most generous and ardent; and the genii who preside over love carried their vows to the orb of Venus.

The women returned to Ogul's castle without having found anything. Zadig, having obtained an introduction, addressed him to this effect:

"May immortal health descend from heaven to guard and keep you all your days! I am a physician, and am come to you in haste on hearing the report of your sickness, and I have brought you a cock-atrice stewed in rose-water. I have no matrimonial intentions with regard to you; I only ask for the release of a young female slave from Babylon, who has been several days in your possession, and I consent to remain in bondage in her place if I have not the happiness of cur-ing the magnificent lord Ogul."

The proposal was accepted. Astarte set out for Babylon with Zadig's servant, having promised to send him a messenger immediately to inform him of all that might have happened. Their parting was as tender as their unexpected recognition. The moment of separation and the moment of meeting again are the two most important epochs of life, as is written in the great book of Zendavesta. Zadig loved the queen as much as he swore he did, and the queen loved Zadig more than she professed to do.

Meanwhile Zadig spoke thus to Ogul:

"My lord, my cockatrice is not to be eaten, all its virtue must enter into you through the pores. I have put it into a little leathern case, well blown out, and covered with a fine skin; you must strike this case of leather as hard as you can, and I must send it back each time; a few days of this treatment will show you what my art can do."

The first day Ogul was quite out of breath, and thought that he should die of fatigue. The second day he was less exhausted, and slept better. In a week's time he had gained all the strength, health, lightness, and good spirits of his most robust years.

"You have played at ball, and you have been temperate," said Zadig; "believe me, there is no such creature in nature as a cockatrice, but with temperance and exercise one is always well, and the art of combining intemperance and health is as chimerical as the philosopher's stone, judicial astrology, and the theology of the magi."

Ogul's former physician, perceiving how dangerous this man was to the cause of medicine, conspired with his private apothecary to dispatch Zadig to hunt for cockatrices in the other world. Thus, after having already been punished so often for having done good, he was again nearly perishing for having healed a gluttonous nobleman. He was invited to a grand dinner and was to have been poisoned during the second course, but while they were at the first he received a message from the fair Astarte, at which he left the table, and took his departure. "When one is loved by a beautiful woman," says the great Zoroaster, "one is always extricated from every scrape."

Chapter 19

The Tournament

THE QUEEN HAD been received at Babylon with the enthusiasm which is always shown for a beautiful princess who has been unfortunate. Babylon at that time seemed more peaceful. The prince of Hyrcania had been killed in a battle, and the victorious Babylonians declared that Astarte should marry the man whom they might elect for monarch. They did not desire that the first position in the world, namely, that of being husband of Astarte and king of Babylon, should depend upon intrigues and cabals. They took an oath to acknowledge as their king the man whom they should find bravest and wisest. Spacious lists, surrounded by an amphitheater splendidly decorated, were

formed at a distance of several leagues from the city. The combatants
were to repair thither armed at all points. Each of them had separate
quarters behind the amphitheater, where he was to be neither seen
nor visited by anyone. It was necessary to enter the lists four times,
and those who should be successful enough to defeat four cavaliers
were thereupon to fight against each other, and the one who should
finally remain master of the field should be proclaimed victor of the
tournament. He was to return four days afterwards with the same
arms, and try to solve the riddles which the magi would propound.
If he could not solve the riddles, he was not to be king, and it would
be necessary to begin the jousts over again until a knight should be
found victorious in both sorts of contest; for they wished to have a
king braver and wiser than any other man. The queen, during all
this time, was to be strictly guarded; she was only allowed to be
present at the games covered with a veil, and she was not permitted
to speak to any of the competitors, in order to avoid either favoritism
or injustice.

This was the intelligence that Astarte sent her lover, hoping that
for her sake he would display greater valor and wisdom than anyone
else. So he took his departure, entreating Venus to fortify his courage
and enlighten his mind. He arrived on the banks of the Euphrates
the evening before the great day, and caused his device to be inscribed
among those of the combatants, concealing his countenance and his
name, as the law required. Then he went to take repose in the lodging
that was assigned him by lot. His friend Cador, who had returned to
Babylon after having vainly searched for him in Egypt, dispatched
to his quarters a complete suit of armor which was the queen's present.
He also sent him, on her behalf, the finest steed in Persia. Zadig
recognized the hand of Astarte in these gifts; his courage and his love
gained thereby new energy and new hopes.

On the morrow, the queen having taken her place under a jeweled
canopy and the amphitheater being filled with ladies and persons of
every rank in Babylon, the combatants appeared in the arena. Each
of them came and laid his device at the feet of the grand magian.
The devices were drawn by lot, and Zadig's happened to be the
last. The first who advanced was a very rich lord named Itobad,
exceedingly vain, but with little courage, skill, or judgment. His
servants had persuaded him that such a man as he ought to be king;
and he had answered them: "Such a man as I ought to reign." So
they had armed him from head to foot. He had golden armor enameled
with green, a green plume, and a lance decked with green ribbons.

It was evident at once, from the manner in which Itobad managed his horse, that it was not for *such a man as he* that heaven reserved the scepter of Babylon. The first knight who tilted against him unhorsed him; the second upset him so that he lay on his horse's crupper with both his legs in the air and arms extended. Itobad recovered his seat, but in such an ungainly fashion that all the spectators began to laugh. The third did not condescend to use his lance, but after making a pass at him, took him by the right leg, turned him half round, and let him drop on the sand. The squires of the tourney ran up to him laughing, and replaced him on his saddle. The fourth combatant seized him by the left leg, and made him fall on the other side. He was accompanied with loud jeers to his quarters, where he was to pass the night according to the law of the games; and he said as he limped along with difficulty: "What an experience for such a man as I!"

The other knights acquitted themselves better. There were some who defeated two antagonists one after the other, a few went as far as three, but the prince Otame was the only one who conquered four. At last Zadig tilted in his turn; he unseated four cavaliers in succession in the most graceful manner possible. It then remained to be seen whether Otame or Zadig would be the victor. The arms of the former were blue and gold, with a plume of the same color, while those of Zadig were white. The sympathies of all were divided between the knight in blue and the knight in white. The queen, whose heart was throbbing violently, put up prayers to heaven that the white might be the winning color.

The two champions made passes and wheeled round with such agility, they delivered such dexterous thrusts, and sat so firmly on their saddles, that all the spectators, except the queen, wished that there might be two kings in Babylon. At last, their chargers being exhausted, and their lances broken, Zadig had recourse to this stratagem: he steps behind the blue prince, leaps upon the crupper of his horse, seizes him by the waist, hurls him down, takes his place in the saddle, and prances round Otame, as he lies stretched upon the ground. All the amphitheater shouts: "Victory to the white cavalier!" Otame rises, indignant at his disgrace, and draws his sword; Zadig springs off the horse's back, saber in hand. Then, lo and behold! both of them on foot in the arena begin a new conflict, in which strength and agility by turns prevail. The plumes of their helmets, the rivets of their arm-pieces, the links of their armor, fly far afield under a thousand rapid blows. With point and edge they thrust and cut, to right and left, now on the head, and now on the chest; they retreat, they advance, they measure swords, they come to close quarters, they wrestle, they twine like serpents, they attack each other like lions; sparks are sent forth every moment from their clashing swords. At last Zadig, recovering his coolness for an instant, stops, makes a feint, and then rushes upon Otame, brings him to the ground, and disarms him, when the vanquished prince exclaims: "O white cavalier, you it is who should reign over Babylon."

The queen's joy was at its climax. The cavalier in blue and the cavalier in white were conducted each to his own lodging, as well as all the others, in due accordance with the law. Mutes came to attend them and to bring them food. It may be easily guessed that the queen's little mute was the one who waited on Zadig. Then they were left to sleep alone until the morning of the next day, when the conqueror was to bring his device to the grand magian to be compared with the roll, and to make himself known.

In spite of his love Zadig slept soundly enough, so tired was he. Itobad, who lay near him, did not sleep a wink. He rose in the night, entered Zadig's quarters, took away his white arms and his device, and left his own green armor in their place. As soon as it was daylight, he went up boldly to the grand magian, and announced that such a man as he was victor. This was unexpected, but his success was proclaimed while Zadig was still asleep. Astarte, surprised, and with despair at her heart, returned to Babylon. The whole amphitheater was already almost empty when Zadig awoke; he looked for his arms, and found only the green armor. He was obliged to put it on, having nothing else near him. Astonished and indignant, he armed himself in a rage, and stepped forth in that guise.

All the people who were left in the amphitheater and arena greeted him with jeers. They pressed round him and insulted him to his face. Never did man endure such bitter mortification. He lost patience, and with his drawn sword dispersed the mob which dared to molest him; but he knew not what course to adopt. He could not see the queen, nor could he lay claim to the white armor which she had sent him, without compromising her; so that, while she was plunged in grief, he was tortured with rage and perplexity. He walked along the banks of the Euphrates, convinced that his star had marked him out for inevitable misery, reviewing in his mind all the misfortunes he had suffered, since his experience of the woman who hated one-eyed men up to this present loss of his armor.

"See what comes," said he, "of awaking too late; if I had slept less, I should now be king of Babylon and husband of Astarte. Knowledge, good conduct and courage have never served to bring me anything but trouble."

At last, murmurs against Providence escaped him, and he was tempted to believe that the world was governed by a cruel destiny, which oppressed the good, and brought prosperity to cavaliers in green. One of his worst grievances was to be obliged to wear that green armor which drew such ridicule upon him; and he sold it to a passing merchant at a low price, taking in exchange from the merchant a gown and a nightcap. In this garb he paced beside the Euphrates, filled with despair, and secretly accusing Providence for always persecuting him.

Chapter 20

The Hermit[10]

WHILE WALKING THUS, Zadig met a hermit, whose white and venerable beard descended to his girdle. He held in his hand a book which he was reading attentively. Zadig stopped, and made him a profound obeisance. The hermit returned his salutation with an air so noble and attractive, that Zadig had the curiosity to enter into conversation with him. He asked him what book he was reading.

"It is the book of destiny," said the hermit; "do you desire to read aught therein?"

He placed the book in Zadig's hands, but he, learned as he was in several languages, could not decipher a single character in the book. This increased his curiosity yet more.

"You seem to me much vexed," said the good father.

"Alas, and with only too much reason!" answered Zadig.

"If you will allow me to accompany you," rejoined the old man, "perhaps I may be of service to you; I have sometimes poured consolation into the souls of the unhappy."

The hermit's aspect, his beard, and his book, inspired Zadig with respect. He found in conversing with him the light of a superior mind. The hermit spoke of destiny, of justice, of morality, of the chief good, of human frailty, of virtue and of vice with an eloquence so lively and touching, that Zadig felt himself drawn towards him by an irresistible charm. He earnestly besought him not to leave him, until they should return to Babylon.

"I myself ask the same favor of you," said the old man; "swear to me by Ormuzd that you will not part from me for some days to come, whatever I may do."

Zadig swore not to do so, and they set out together.

The two travelers arrived that evening at a magnificent castle, where the hermit craved hospitality for himself and for the young man who accompanied him. The porter, who might have been taken for a distinguished nobleman, introduced them with a sort of disdainful politeness. They were presented to one of the principal domestics, who showed them the master's splendid apartments. They were admitted to the lower end of his table, without being honored even with a look from the lord of the castle; but they were served like the others, with elegance and profusion. A golden bowl studded with emeralds and rubies was afterwards brought them, wherein to wash their hands. For the night they were consigned to fine sleeping apartments, and in the morning a servant brought each of them a piece of gold, after which they were courteously dismissed.

"The master of the house," said Zadig, when they were again on their way, "seems to me to be a generous man, but a little too proud; he practices a noble hospitality."

As he said these words, he perceived that a very wide sort of pocket which the hermit was wearing appeared stretched and stuffed out, and he caught sight of the golden bowl adorned with precious stones, which the hermit had stolen. He did not at first venture to take any notice of it, but he experienced a strange surprise.

Towards midday, the hermit presented himself at the door of a very small house, inhabited by a very rich miser, of whom he begged hospitable entertainment for a few hours. An old servant, meanly clad, received them roughly, and conducted the hermit and Zadig to the stable, where some rotten olives, moldy bread, and sour beer were given them. The hermit ate and drank with as contented an air as on the evening before; then, turning to the old servant who was watching them both to see that they stole nothing, and who kept urging them to go, he gave him the two pieces of gold which he had received that morning, and thanked him for all his attentions.

"Pray," added he, "let me speak a word to your master."

The astonished servant introduced the two strangers.

"Magnificent lord," said the hermit, "I cannot refrain from offering you my most humble thanks for the noble manner in which you have treated us; deign to accept this golden bowl as a slight token of my gratitude."

The miser almost fell backward from his seat, but the hermit, not giving him time to recover from his sudden surprise, departed with his young companion as quickly as possible.

"Father," said Zadig, "what is all this that I see? You do not seem to me to resemble other men in anything that you do; you steal a bowl adorned with precious stones from a nobleman who entertained you sumptuously, and you give it to a miser who treats you with indignity."

"My son," replied the old man, "that pompous person, who entertains strangers only out of vanity, and to excite admiration of his riches, will learn a needful lesson, while the miser will be taught to practice hospitality; be astonished at nothing, and follow me."

Zadig was still uncertain whether he had to do with a man more foolish or more wise than all other men, but the hermit spoke with a tone of such superiority, that Zadig, bound besides by his oath, felt constrained to follow him.

In the evening they arrived at a house built in a pleasing but simple style, where nothing betokened either prodigality or avarice. The master was a philosopher who, retired from the world, pursued in peace the study of wisdom and virtue, and who, nevertheless, felt life no tedious burden. It had pleased him to build this retreat, into which he welcomed strangers with a generosity which was free from ostentation. He went himself to meet the travelers, and ushered them into a comfortable apartment, where he first left them to repose awhile. Some time afterwards he came in person to invite them to a clean and well-cooked meal, during which he spoke with great good sense about the latest revolutions in Babylon. He seemed sincerely attached to the queen, and expressed a wish that Zadig had appeared in the lists as a competitor for the crown.

"But mankind," added he, "do not deserve to have a king like Zadig."

The latter blushed, and felt his disappointment return with double force. In the course of conversation it was generally agreed that matters in this world do not always fall out as the wisest men would wish. The hermit maintained throughout that we are ignorant of the ways of Providence, and that men are wrong in judging of the whole by the very small part which alone they are able to perceive.

They spoke of the passions. "Ah, how fatal they are!" said Zadig.

"They are the winds that swell the sails of the vessel," replied the hermit; "they sometimes sink the vessel, but it could not make way without them. The bile makes men choleric and sick, but without the bile they could not live. Everything here below has its danger, and yet everything is necessary."

Then they spoke of pleasure, and the hermit proved that it is a gift of the Deity.

"For," said he, "man can give himself neither sensation nor idea, he receives them all; pain and pleasure come to him from without like his very existence."

Zadig marveled how a man who had acted so extravagantly could argue so well. At length, after a discourse as profitable as it was agreeable, their host conducted the two travelers back to their apartment, blessing heaven for having sent him two men so virtuous and so wise; and he offered them money in a frank and easy manner that could give no offense. The hermit, however, refused it, and told him that he must now take leave of him, as he purposed departing for Babylon before morning. Their parting was affectionate; Zadig especially felt full of esteem and love for so amiable a man.

When the hermit and he were alone in their chamber, they passed a long time in praising their host. The old man at daybreak awoke his comrade.

"We must start," said he, "while all the household is asleep. I wish to leave this man a token of my regard and affection."

Saying these words, he seized a light, and set fire to the house. Zadig uttered a cry of horror, and would fain have prevented him from committing so dreadful a deed, but the hermit dragged him away by superior force, and the house was soon in flames. The hermit, who was now at a safe distance with his companion, calmly watched it burning.

"Thank God!" said he; "there goes the house of my dear host, destroyed from basement to roof! Happy man!

At these words Zadig was tempted at once to burst out laughing, to overwhelm the reverend father with reproaches, to beat him, and to fly from him. But he did none of these things; still overawed by the hermit's dominating influence, he followed him in spite of himself to their last quarters for the night.

It was at the house of a charitable and virtuous widow, who had a nephew fourteen years of age, full of engaging qualities, and her only hope. She did the honors of her house as well as she could, and on the morrow she bade her nephew conduct the travelers as far as a bridge which, having broken down a short time before, was now dangerous to cross. The lad walked before them with alacrity. When they were on the bridge, the hermit said to the youth:

"Come, I must prove my gratitude to your aunt."

Then he seized him by the hair and threw him into the river. The boy sank, rose for a moment above the water, and was then swallowed up by the torrent.

"O monster! Most wicked of all mankind!" exclaimed Zadig.

"You promised to be more patient," said the hermit, interrupting him. "Know that under the ruins of that house to which Providence set fire, the master has found an immense treasure; and that this youth, whose neck Providence has twisted, would have murdered his aunt within a year, and yourself within two."

"Savage, who told you so?" cried Zadig; "and though you may have read this event in your book of destiny, are you allowed to drown a child who has done you no harm?"

While the Babylonian was speaking, he perceived that the old man had no longer a beard, and that his countenance assumed the features of youth. The habit of a hermit disappeared; four beautiful wings covered a form majestic and glittering with light.

"O messenger from heaven! Divine angel!" cried Zadig, falling on his knees; "art thou then descended from the empyrean to teach a feeble mortal to submit to the eternal decrees?"

"Mankind," said the angel Jesrad, "judges of everything when knowing nothing; of all men you were the one who most deserved to be enlightened."

Zadig asked if he might have permission to speak.

"I distrust myself," said he, "but may I venture to ask thee to resolve my doubt? Would it not have been better to have corrected this youth, and to have rendered him virtuous, than to have drowned him?"

Jesrad answered: "If he had been virtuous, and had continued to live, it would have been his destiny to be murdered himself, together with the wife he was to marry, and the son whom she was to bear."

"What!" said Zadig, "is it inevitable then that there should be crimes and misfortunes? The misfortunes too, fall upon the good!"

"The wicked," answered Jesrad, "are always unhappy; they serve to try a small number of righteous men scattered over the earth, and there is no evil from which some good does not spring."

"But," said Zadig, "what if there were only good, and no evil at all?"

"Then," answered Jesrad, "this earth would be another world; the chain of events would be ordered by wisdom of another kind; and this order, which would be perfect, can only exist in the eternal abode of the Supreme Being, which evil cannot approach. He has created millions of worlds, not one of which can resemble another. This boundless variety is an attribute of His boundless power. There are not two leaves of a tree upon this earth, nor two globes in the infinite fields of heaven, which are alike, and everything that you see on this little atom where you have been born must fill its own place, and exist in its own fixed time, according to the immutable decrees of Him who embraces all. Men think that this child who has just perished fell into the water by accident, that it was by accident likewise that that house was burned; but there is no such thing as accident; all that takes place is either a trial, or a punishment, or a reward, or a providential dispensation. Remember that fisherman who deemed himself the most miserable of men. Ormuzd sent you to change his destiny. Feeble mortal, cease to dispute against that which it is your duty to adore."

"But," said Zadig.

As the word was on his lips, the angel was already winging his way towards the tenth sphere. Zadig on his knees adored Providence, and was resigned. The angel cried to him from on high:

"Take your way towards Babylon."

Chapter 21

The Riddles

ZADIG, IN A state of bewilderment, and like a man at whose side the lightning has fallen, walked on at random. He entered Babylon on the day when those who had contended in the lists were already assembled in the grand vestibule of the palace to solve the riddles, and to answer the questions of the grand magian. All the knights were there, except him of the green armor. As soon as Zadig appeared in the city, the people gathered round him; they could not satisfy their eyes with the sight of him, their mouths with blessing him, or their hearts with wishing him to be king. The Envious man saw him pass, trembled, and turned aside, while the people escorted him to the place of assembly. The queen, to whom his arrival was announced, became a prey to the agitation of fear and hope; she was devoured with uneasiness, and could not comprehend why Zadig was unarmed, and how it came to pass that Itobad wore the white armor. A confused murmur arose at the sight of Zadig. All were surprised and delighted to see him again; but only the knights who had taken part in the tournament were permitted to appear in the assembly.

"I have fought like the others," said he; "but another here wears my armor, and, while I must wait to have the honor of proving it, I ask leave to present myself in order to explain the riddles."

The question was put to the vote; his reputation for integrity was still so deeply impressed on the minds of all, that there was no hesitation about admitting him.

The grand magian first proposed this question:

"What, of all things in the world, is alike the longest and the shortest, the quickest and the slowest, the most minutely divided and the most widely extended, the most neglected and the most regretted, without which nothing can be done, which devours everything that is little, and confers life on everything that is great?"

Itobad was to speak first; he answered that such a man as he understood nothing about riddles, that it was enough for him to have conquered by the might of his arm. Some said that the answer to the riddle was fortune; according to others it was the earth, and according to others again light. Zadig said that it was time:

"Nothing is longer," added he, "since it is the measure of eternity; nothing is shorter, since it fails to accomplish our projects. There is nothing slower to one who waits, nothing quicker to one who enjoys. It extends to infinity in greatness, it is infinitely divisible in minuteness. All men neglect it, all regret its loss. Nothing is done without it. It buries in oblivion all that is unworthy of being handed down to posterity; and it confers immortality upon all things that are great."

The assembly agreed that Zadig's answer was the right one.

The next question was:

"What is it which we receive without acknowledgment, which we enjoy without knowing how, which we bestow on others when we know nothing about it, and which we lose without perceiving the loss?"

Everybody had his own explanation. Zadig alone guessed that it was life, and explained all the other riddles with the same readiness. Itobad said on each occasion that nothing was easier and that he would have come to the same conclusion with equal facility if he had cared to give himself the trouble. Questions were afterwards propounded on justice, the chief good, and the art of government. Zadig's replies were pronounced the soundest.

"What a pity," it was said, "that one whose judgment is so good should be so bad a knight!"

"Illustrious lords," said Zadig, "I have had the honor of conquering in the lists. It is to me that the white armor belongs. The lord Itobad possessed himself of it while I slept; he thought, apparently, that it would become him better than the green. I am ready to prove upon his person forthwith before you all, in this garb and armed only with my sword, against all this fine white armor which he has stolen from me, that it was I who had the honor of vanquishing brave Otame."

Itobad accepted the challenge with the greatest confidence. He felt no doubt that, armed as he was with helmet, breastplate, and brassarts, he would soon see the last of a champion arrayed in a nightcap and a dressing gown. Zadig drew his sword, and saluted the queen, who gazed on him with the deepest emotion of mingled joy and alarm. Itobad unsheathed his weapon without saluting anyone. He advanced upon Zadig like a man who had nothing to fear, and made ready to cleave his head open. Zadig adroitly parried the stroke, opposing the strongest part of his sword to the weakest part of that of his adversary in such a way that Itobad's blade was broken. Then Zadig, seizing his enemy round the waist, hurled him to the ground, and, holding the point of his sword where the breastplate ended, said:

"Submit to be disarmed, or I take your life."

Itobad, who was always surprised at any disgrace which befell such a man as he, suffered Zadig to do what he pleased, who peaceably relieved him of his splendid helmet, his superb breastplate, his fine brassarts, and his glittering thigh-pieces, put them on himself again, and ran in this array to throw himself at Astarte's knees.

Cador had no difficulty in proving that the armor belonged to Zadig. He was acknowledged king by unanimous consent, and most of all by Astarte, who tasted, after so many adversities, the delight of seeing her lover regarded by all the world as worthy of being her husband. Itobad went away to hear himself called his lordship in his own house. Zadig was made king, and he was happy. What the angel Jesrad had said to him was present to his mind, and he even remembered the grain of sand which became a diamond. The queen and he together adored Providence. Zadig left the beautiful and capricious Missouf to range the world at will. He sent in search of the brigand Arbogad, gave him an honorable post in his army, and promised to promote him to the highest rank if he behaved himself like a true warrior, but threatened to have him hanged, if he followed the trade of a robber.

Setoc was summoned from the heart of Arabia, together with the fair Almona, and set at the head of the commerce of Babylon. Cador was loved and honored, receiving an appointment such as his services deserved; he was the king's friend, and Zadig was then the only monarch upon earth who had one. The little mute was not forgotten. A fine house was given to the fisherman, while Orcan was condemned to pay him a large sum and to give him back his wife; but the fisherman, now grown wise, took the money only.

The fair Semira was inconsolable for having believed that Zadig would be blind of an eye; and Azora never ceased lamenting that she had wished to cut off his nose. He soothed their sorrow with presents. The Envious man died of rage and shame. The empire enjoyed peace, glory, and abundance; that age was the best which the earth had known, for it was ruled by justice and by love. All men blessed Zadig, and Zadig blessed heaven.

[The manuscript containing Zadig's history ends here. We know that he experienced many other adventures which have been faithfully recorded. Interpreters of oriental tongues are requested, if they should meet with any such records, to make them public.]

MICROMÉGAS

A PHILOSOPHICAL TALE

Chapter 1

Journey of an Inhabitant of the System of the Star Sirius to the Planet Saturn

IN ONE OF those planets which revolve round the star named Sirius there lived a young man of great intelligence, whose acquaintance I had the honor of making on the occasion of his last journey to our little ant-hill. He was called Micromégas,[1] a name which is exceedingly appropriate to all great people. He had a stature of eight leagues, and by eight leagues I mean twenty-four thousand geometrical paces of five feet each.

Here some mathematicians, a class of persons who are always useful to the public, will immediately take up the pen, and find out by calculation that since Mr. Micromégas, inhabitant of the country of Sirius, is twenty-four thousand paces in height from head to foot, which make one hundred and twenty thousand statute feet, whereas we denizens of the earth have an average stature of hardly more than five feet, and, since our globe is nine thousand leagues in circumference, they will find, I say, that the world which produced him must have a circumference precisely twenty-one millions six hundred thousand times greater than our little earth. Nothing in nature is simpler, more a matter of course. The dominions of certain potentates in Germany or Italy, round which you can walk in half an hour, as compared with the empire of Turkey, of Russia, or of China, can give but a very faint idea of the prodigious differences which nature has set between various orders of being throughout the universe.

His Excellency's height being what I have said, all our sculptors and painters will readily agree that his waist may be about fifty thousand feet round, which would constitute a symmetrical proportion. His nose being one-third of the length of his handsome face, and his handsome face being the seventh part of the height of his handsome body, it will indisputably follow that the Sirian's nose is six thousand three hundred and thirty-three statute feet in length, and a fraction more; which was the proposition to be proved.

As to his mind, it is worthy to rank with the most cultivated among us; he knows many things, some of which are of his own invention. He had not yet reached his two hundred and fiftieth year, and was studying, as was customary at his age, at the most famous school in the planet, when he solved, by the strength of his own intellect, more than fifty propositions of Euclid, that is, eighteen more than Blaise Pascal, who, after having, according to his sister's account, solved thirty-two for his own amusement, afterwards became a pretty fair geometer, and a very poor metaphysician. When he was about four hundred and fifty years of age, and already passing out of childhood, he dissected a great many little insects less than a hundred feet in diameter, such as are invisible under ordinary microscopes, and composed a very curious book about them, but one which brought him into some trouble. The mufti of that country, much given to hair-splitting and very ignorant, found in his work statements which he deemed suspicious, offensive, rash, heretical or savoring of heresy, and he prosecuted him for it with the bitterest animosity. The question in dispute was whether the substantial form of which the fleas of Sirius consisted was of the same nature as that of the snails. Micromégas defended himself with spirit, and had all the ladies on his side; the trial lasted two hundred and twenty years. At last the mufti had the book condemned by judges who had never read it, and the author was forbidden to appear at court for eight hundred years.

He was only moderately afflicted at being banished from a court which was full of nothing but trickery and meanness. He composed a very funny song in ridicule of the mufti, which in its turn failed to give the latter much annoyance;[2] and he himself set forth on his travels from planet to planet, with a view to improving his mind and soul, as the saying is. Those who travel only in postchaises or family coaches, will doubtless be astonished at the sort of conveyance adopted up there; for we, on our little mound of mud, can imagine nothing that surpasses our own experience. Our traveler had such a marvelous acquaintance with the laws of gravitation, and with all the forces of attraction and repulsion, and made such good use of his knowledge, that, sometimes by means of a sunbeam, and sometimes by the help of a comet, he and his companions went from one world to another as a bird hops from bough to bough. He traversed the Milky Way in a very short time; and I am obliged to confess that he never saw, beyond the stars with which it is thickly sown, that beautiful celestial empyrean which the illustrious parson, Derham[2] boasts of having discovered at the end of his telescope. Not that I would for a moment suggest that Mr. Derham mistook what he saw; heaven forbid! But Micromégas was on the spot, he is an accurate observer, and I have no wish to contradict anybody. Micromégas, after plenty of turns and twists, arrived at the planet Saturn. Accustomed though he was to the sight of novelties, when he saw the insignificant size of the globe and its inhabitants, he could not at first refrain from that smile of superiority which sometimes escapes even the wisest; for in truth Saturn is scarcely nine hundred times greater than the earth, and the citizens of that country are mere dwarfs, only a thousand fathoms high, or thereabout. He laughed a little at first at these people, in much the same way as an Italian musician, when he comes to France, is wont to deride Lulli's performances. But, as the Sirian was a sensible fellow, he was very soon convinced that a thinking being need not be altogether ridiculous because he is no more than six thousand feet high. He was soon on familiar terms with the Saturnians after their astonishment had somewhat subsided. He formed an intimate friendship with the secretary of the Academy of Saturn, a man of great intelligence, who had not indeed invented anything himself, but was a capital hand at describing the inventions of others, and one who could turn a little verse neatly enough or perform an elaborate calculation. I will here introduce, for the gratification of my readers, a singular conversation that Micromégas one day held with Mr. Secretary.

Chapter 2

Conversation between an Inhabitant of Sirius and a Native of Saturn

AFTER HIS EXCELLENCY had laid himself down, and the secretary had approached his face, Micromégas said:

"I must needs confess that nature is full of variety."

"Yes," said the Saturnian; "nature is like a flowerbed, the blossoms of which—"

"Oh," said the other, "have done with your flowerbed!"

"She is," resumed the secretary, "like an assembly of blondes and brunettes, whose attire——"

"Pooh! What have I to do with your brunettes?" said the other.

"She is like a gallery of pictures, then, the outlines of which——"

"No, no," said the traveler; "once more, nature is like nature. Why do you search for comparisons?"

"To please you," answered the secretary.

"I do not want to be pleased," rejoined the traveler; "I want to be instructed: begin by telling me how many senses the men in your world possess?"

"We have seventy-two," said the academician; "and we are always complaining that they are so few. Our imagination goes beyond our needs; we find that with our seventy-two senses, our ring, and our five moons, our range is too restricted, and, in spite of all our curiosity and the tolerably large number of passions which spring out of our seventy-two senses, we have plenty of time to feel bored."

"I can well believe it," said Micromégas; "for in our globe, although we have nearly a thousand senses, there lingers even in us a certain vague desire, an unaccountable restlessness, which warns us unceasingly that we are of little account in the universe, and that there are beings much more perfect than ourselves. I have traveled a little; I have seen mortals far below us, and others as greatly superior; but I have seen none who have not more desires than real wants, and more wants than they can satisfy. I shall some day, perhaps, reach the country where there is lack of nothing, but hitherto no one has been able to give me any positive information about it." The Saturnian and the Sirian thereupon exhausted themselves in conjectures on the subject, but after a great deal of argumentative discussion, as ingenious as it was futile, they were obliged to return to facts.

"How long do you people live?" asked the Sirian.

"Ah, a very short time," replied the little man of Saturn.

"That is just the way with us," said the Sirian; "we are always complaining of the shortness of life. This must be a universal law of nature."

"Alas," quoth the Saturnian, "none of us lives for more than five hundred annual revolutions of the sun;"——that amounts to about fifteen thousand years, according to our manner of counting——"you see how it is our fate to die almost as soon as we are born: our existence is a point, our duration an instant, our globe an atom. Scarcely have we begun to acquire a little information when death arrives before we can put it to use. For my part, I do not venture to lay any schemes; I feel myself like a drop of water in a boundless ocean. I am ashamed, especially before you, of the absurd figure I make in this universe."

Micromégas answered: "If you were not a philosopher, I should fear to distress you by telling you that our lives are seven hundred times as long as yours, but you know too well that when the time comes to give back one's body to the elements and to reanimate nature under another form, which process is called death,—when that moment of metamorphosis comes, it is precisely the same thing whether we have lived an eternity or only a day. I have been in countries where life is a thousand times longer than with us, and yet have heard murmurs at its brevity even there. But people of good sense are to be found everywhere who know how to make the most of what they have, and to thank the Author of nature. He has spread over this universe abundant variety, together with a kind of admirable uniformity. For example, all thinking beings are different, yet they all resemble each other essentially in the common endowment of thought and will. Matter is infinitely extended, but it has different properties in different worlds. How many of these various properties do you reckon in the matter with which you are acquainted?"

"If you speak," replied the Saturnian, "of those properties without which we believe that this globe could not subsist as it is, we reckon three hundred of them, such as extension, impenetrability, mobility, gravitation, divisibility, and so on."

"Apparently," rejoined the traveler, "this small number is sufficient for the purpose which the Creator had in view in constructing this little habitation. I admire His wisdom throughout; I see differences everywhere, but everywhere also a due proportion. Your globe is small, you who inhabit it are small likewise; you have few senses, the matter of which your world consists has few properties; all this is the work of Providence. Of what color is your sun when carefully examined?"

"White deeply tinged with yellow," said the Saturnian; "and when we split up one of its rays, we find that it consists of seven colors."

"Our sun has a reddish light," said the Sirian, "and we have thirty-nine primitive colors. There is not a single sun, among all those that I have approached, which resembles any other, just as among yourselves there is not a single face which is not different from all the rest."

After several other questions of this kind, he inquired how many essentially different modes of existence were enumerated in Saturn. He was told that not more than thirty were distinguished, as God, space, matter, beings occupying space which feel and think, thinking beings which do not occupy space, those which possess penetrability, others which do not do so, etc. The Sirian, in whose world they count three hundred of them, and who had discovered three thousand more in the course of his travels, astonished the philosopher of Saturn immensely. At length, after having communicated to each other a little of what they knew, and a great deal of that about which they knew nothing, and after having exercised their reasoning powers during a complete revolution of the sun, they resolved to make a little philosophical tour together.

Chapter 3

The Sirian and the Saturnian as Fellow Travelers

OUR TWO PHILOSOPHERS were ready to embark upon the atmosphere of Saturn, with a fine collection of mathematical instruments, when the Saturnian's mistress, who got wind of what he was going to do, came in tears to remonstrate with him. She was a pretty little brunette, whose stature did not exceed six hundred and sixty fathoms, but her agreeable manners amply atoned for that deficiency.

"Oh, cruel one!" she exclaimed, "after having resisted you for fifteen hundred years, and when I was at last beginning to surrender, and have passed scarcely a hundred years in your arms, to leave me thus and start on a long journey with a giant of another world! Go, you have no taste for anything but novelty, you have never felt what it is to love! If you were a true Saturnian, you would be constant. Whither away so fast? What is it you would have? Our five moons are less fickle than you, our ring is less changeable. So much for what is past! I will never love anyone again."

The philosopher embraced her, and, in spite of all his philosophy, joined his tears with hers. As to the lady, after having fainted away, she proceeded to console herself with a certain beau who lived in the neighborhood.

Meanwhile our two inquirers set forth on their travels; they first of all jumped upon Saturn's ring, which they found pretty flat, as an illustrious inhabitant of our little globe has very cleverly conjectured;[3] thence they easily made their way from moon to moon. A comet passed quite near the last one, so they sprang upon it, together with their servants and their instruments. When they had gone about a hundred and fifty millions of leagues, they came across the satellites of Jupiter. They landed on Jupiter itself, and remained there for a year, during which they learned some very remarkable secrets which would be at the present moment in the press, were it not for the gentlemen who act as censors, and who have discovered therein some statements too hard for them to swallow. But I have read the manuscript which contains them in the library of the illustrious Archbishop of—, who, with a generosity and kindness which cannot be sufficiently commended, has permitted me to peruse his books. Accordingly I promise to give him a long article in the next edition that shall be brought out of Moreri,[4] and I will be specially careful not to forget his sons, who afford such good hope of the perpetuation of their illustrious father's progeny.

But let us return to our travelers. Quitting Jupiter, they traversed a space of about a hundred million leagues, and, coasting along the planet Mars, which, as is well known, is five times smaller than our own little globe, they saw two moons, which attend upon that planet, and which have escaped the observation of our astronomers. I am well aware that Father Castel will write, and pleasantly enough too, against the existence of these two moons, but I refer myself to those who reason from analogy. Those excellent philosophers know how difficult it would be for Mars, which is such a long way off from the sun, to get on with less than two moons. Be that as it may, our friends found the planet so small, that they were afraid of finding no room there to put up for the night, so they proceeded on their way, like a pair of travelers who disdain a humble village inn, and push on to the nearest town. But the Sirian and his companion soon had cause to repent having done so, for they went on for a long time without finding anything at all. At last they perceived a faint glimmer; it came from our earth, and created compassion in the minds of those who had so lately left Jupiter. However, for fear of repenting a second time, they decided to disembark. They passed over the tail of the comet, and meeting with an aurora borealis close at hand, they got inside, and alighted on the earth by the northern shore of the Baltic Sea, July the 5th, 1737, new style.

Chapter 4

What Happened to the Travelers on the Terrestrial Globe

AFTER HAVING RESTED for some time, they consumed for their breakfast a couple of mountains, which their people prepared for them as daintily as possible. Then, wishing to inspect the country where they were, they first went from north to south. Each of the Sirian's ordinary steps was about thirty thousand statute feet; the Saturnian dwarf, whose height was only a thousand fathoms, followed panting far behind, for he had to take about a dozen steps when the other made a single stride. Picture to yourself (if I may be allowed to make such a comparison) a tiny little toy spaniel pursuing a captain of the King of Prussia's grenadiers.

As the strangers proceeded pretty quickly, they made the circuit of the globe in thirty-six hours; the sun, indeed, or rather the earth, makes the same journey in a day, but it must be borne in mind that it is a much easier way of getting on, to turn on one's axis, than to walk on one's feet. Behold our travelers, then, returned to the same spot from which they had started, after having set eyes upon that sea, to them almost imperceptible, which is called the Mediterranean, and that other little pond which, under the name of the great Ocean, surrounds this mole-hill. Therein the dwarf had never sunk much above the knee, while the other had scarcely wetted his ankle. They did all they could, searching here and there, both when going and returning, to ascertain whether the earth were inhabited or not. They stooped, they lay down, they groped about in all directions; but their eyes and their hands being out of all proportion to the tiny beings who crawl up and down here, they felt not the slightest sensation which could lead them to suspect that we and our fellow creatures, the other inhabitants of this globe, have the honor to exist.

The dwarf, who sometimes judged a little too hastily, at once decided that there was not a single creature on the earth. His first reason was that he had not seen one. But Micromégas politely gave him to understand that that was not a good argument:

"For," said he, "you, with your little eyes, cannot see certain stars of the fiftieth magnitude which I distinctly discern; do you conclude from that circumstance that those stars have no existence?"

"But," said the dwarf, "I have felt about very carefully."

"But," rejoined the other, "your powers of perception may be at fault."

"But," continued the dwarf, "this globe is so ill-constructed, it is so irregular, and, it seems to me, of so ridiculous a shape! All here appears to be in a state of chaos: look at these little brooks, not one of which goes in a straight line; look at these ponds, which are neither round nor square, nor oval, nor of any regular form; and all these little sharp-pointed grains with which this globe bristles, and which have rubbed the skin off my feet!"—he alluded to the mountains—"Observe too the shape of the globe as a whole, how it is flat at the poles, how it turns round the sun in a clumsily slanting manner, so that the polar climes are necessarily mere wastes. In truth, what chiefly makes me think that there is nobody here, is that I cannot suppose any people of sense would wish to occupy such a dwelling."

"Well," said Micromégas, "perhaps the people who inhabit it are not people of sense. But in point of fact there are some signs of its not having been made for nothing. Everything here seems to you irregular, you say; that is because everything is judged by the measures of Saturn and Jupiter. Ay, perhaps it is for that very reason that there is so much apparent confusion here. Have I not told you that in the course of my travels I have always remarked the presence of variety?"

The Saturnian had answers to meet all these arguments, and the dispute might never have ended, if Micromégas, in the heat of discussion, had not luckily broken the thread which bound together his collar of diamonds, so that they fell to the ground; pretty little stones they were, of rather unequal size, the largest of which weighed four hundred pounds, and the smallest not more than fifty. The dwarf, who picked up some of them, perceived, on bringing them near his eyes, that these diamonds, from the fashion in which they were cut, made capital microscopes. He accordingly took up a little magnifier of one hundred and sixty feet in diameter, which he applied to his eye; and Micromégas selected one of two thousand five hundred feet across. They were of high power, but at first nothing was revealed by their help, so the focus had to be adjusted. At last the inhabitant of Saturn saw something almost imperceptible which moved half under water in the Baltic sea; it was a whale. He caught it very cleverly with his little finger, and, placing it on his thumb nail, showed it to the Sirian, who burst out laughing a second time at the extreme minuteness of the inhabitants of our system. The Saturnian, now convinced that our world was inhabited, immediately rushed to the conclusion that whales were the only creatures to be found there; and, as speculation was his strong point, he pleased himself with conjectures as to the origin of so insignificant an atom and the source of its movement, whether it had ideas and free will. Micromégas was a good deal puzzled about it; he examined the creature very patiently, and the result of his investigation was that he had no grounds for supposing that it had a soul lodged in its body. The two travelers then were inclined to think that there was no being possessed of intelligence in this habitation of ours, when with the aid of the microscope they detected something as big as a whale, floating on the Baltic sea. We know that at that very time a flock of philosophers were returning from the polar circle, whither they had gone to make observations which no one had attempted before. The newspapers say that their vessel ran aground in the gulf of Bothnia, and that they had great difficulty in saving their lives; but we never know in this world the real truth about anything. I am going to relate honestly what took place, without adding anything of my own invention, a task which demands no small effort on the part of an historian.

Chapter 5

Experiences and Conjectures of the Two Travelers

MICROMÉGAS STRETCHED OUT his hand very gently towards the place where the object appeared. Thrusting forward two fingers, he quickly drew them back lest his hopes should be defeated; then, cautiously opening and closing them, he seized with great dexterity the ship which carried those gentlemen, and placed it likewise on his nail without squeezing it too much, for fear of crushing it.

"Here is an animal quite different from the first," said the Saturnian dwarf. The Sirian placed the supposed animal in the hollow of his hand. The passengers and crew, who thought that they had been whirled aloft by a tempest and supposed that they had struck upon some kind of rock, began to bestir themselves; the sailors seized casks of wine, threw them overboard on Micromégas's hand, and afterwards jumped down themselves, while the geometers seized their quadrants, their sectors, and a pair of Lapland girls, and descended on the Sirian's fingers. They made such a commotion, that at last he felt something tickling him; it was a pole with an iron point being driven a foot deep into his forefinger. He judged from this prick that it had proceeded somehow from the little animal that he was holding; but at first he perceived nothing more. The magnifier, which scarcely enabled them to discern a whale and a ship, had no effect upon a being so insignificant as man. I have no wish to shock the vanity of anyone, but here I am obliged to beg those who are sensitive about their own importance to consider what I have to say on this subject. Taking the average stature of mankind at five feet, we make no greater figure on the earth than an insect not quite the six hundred thousandth part of an inch in height would do upon a bowl ten feet round. Figure to yourselves a being who could hold the earth in his hand, and who had organs of sense proportionate to our own,— and it may well be conceived that there are a great number of such beings,—consider then, I pray you, what they would think of those battles which give the conqueror possession of some village, to be lost again soon afterwards.

I have no doubt that if some captain of tall grenadiers ever reads this work, he will raise the caps of his company at least a couple of feet; but I warn him that it will be all in vain, that he and his men will never be anything but the merest mites.

What marvelous skill then must our philosopher from Sirius have possessed in order to perceive those atoms of which I have been speaking! When Leuwenhoek and Hartsoeker first saw, or thought they saw, the minute speck out of which we are formed, they did not make nearly so surprising a discovery.[5] What pleasure then did Micromégas feel in watching the movements of those little machines, in examining all their feats, in following all their operations! How he shouted for joy, as he placed one of his microscopes in his companion's hand!

"I see them," they exclaimed both at once; "do you not observe how they are carrying burdens, how they stoop down and rise up?"

As they spoke, their hands trembled with delight at beholding objects so unusual, and with fear lest they might lose them. The Saturnian, passing from the one extreme of skepticism to an equal degree of credulity, fancied that he saw them engaged in the work of propagation.

"Ah!" said he, "I have surprised nature in the very act."[6]

But he was deceived by appearances, an accident to which we are only too liable, whether we make use of microscopes or not.

Chapter 6

What Communication They Held with Men

MICROMÉGAS, A MUCH better observer than his dwarf, perceived clearly that the atoms were speaking to each other, and he called his companion's attention to the circumstance; but he, ashamed as he was of having made a mistake on the subject of generation, was indisposed to believe that such creatures as they could have any means of communicating ideas. He had the gift of tongues as well as the Sirian; he did not hear the atoms speak, so he concluded that they did not do so. Besides, how could those imperceptible beings have vocal organs, and what could they have to say? To be able to speak, one must think, or at least make some approach to thought; but if those creatures could think, then they must have something equivalent to a soul; now to attribute the equivalent of a soul to these little animals appeared to him absurd.

"But," said the Sirian, "you fancied just now that they were making love; do you imagine that they can make love without being able to think or utter a word, or even to make themselves understood? Moreover, do you suppose that it is more difficult to produce arguments than offspring? Both appear to me equally mysterious operations."

"I no longer venture either to believe or to deny," said the dwarf; "I no longer have any opinion about the matter. We must try to examine these insects, we will form our conclusions afterwards."

"That is very well said," replied Micromégas; and he straightway drew forth a pair of scissors with which he cut his nails, and immediately made out of a paring from his thumb nail a sort of monster speaking trumpet, like a huge funnel, the narrow end of which he put into his ear. As the wide part of the funnel included the ship and all her crew, the faintest voice was conveyed along the circular fibers of the nail in such a manner, that, thanks to his perseverance, the philosopher high above them clearly heard the buzzing of our insects down below. In a few hours he succeeded in distinguishing the words, and at last in understanding the French language. The dwarf heard the same, but with more difficulty. The astonishment of the travelers increased every instant. They heard mere mites speaking tolerably good sense; such a freak of nature seemed to them inexplicable. You may imagine how impatiently the Sirian and his dwarf longed to hold conversation with the atoms; but the dwarf was afraid that his voice of thunder, and still more that of Micromégas, might deafen the mites without conveying any meaning. It became necessary to diminish its strength; they, accordingly, placed in their mouths instruments like little toothpicks, the tapering end of which was brought near the ship. Then the Sirian, holding the dwarf on his knees, and the vessel with her crew upon his nail, bent his head down and spoke in a low voice, thus at last, with the help of all these precautions and many others besides, beginning to address them:

"Invisible insects, whom the hand of the Creator has been pleased to produce in the abyss of the infinitely little, I thank Him for having deigned to reveal to me secrets which seemed inscrutable. It may be the courtiers of my country would not condescend to look upon you, but I despise no one, and I offer you my protection."

If ever anyone was astonished, it was the people who heard these words, nor could they guess whence they came. The ship's chaplain repeated the prayers used in exorcism, the sailors swore, and the philosophers constructed theories; but whatever theories they constructed, they could not divine who was speaking to them. The dwarf of Saturn, who had a softer voice than Micromégas, then told them in a few words with what kind of beings they had to do. He gave them an account of the journey from Saturn, and made them acquainted with the parts and powers of Mr. Micromégas; and, after having commiserated them for being so small, he asked them if they had always been in that pitiful condition, little better than annihilation, what they found to do on a globe that appeared to belong to whales, if they were happy, if they increased and multiplied, whether they had souls, and a hundred other questions of that nature.

A philosopher of the party, bolder than the rest of them, and shocked that the existence of his soul should be called in question, took observations of the speaker with a quadrant from two different stations, and, at the third, spoke as follows:

"Do you then suppose, sir, because a thousand fathoms extend between your head and your feet, that you are—"

"A thousand fathoms!" cried the dwarf; "good heavens! How is it that he knows my height? A thousand fathoms! He is not an inch out in his reckoning. What! Has that atom actually measured me? He is a geometer, he knows my size; while I, who cannot see him except through a microscope, am still ignorant of his!'"

"Yes, I have taken your measure," said the man of science; "and I will now proceed, if you please, to measure your big companion."

The proposal was accepted; His Excellency lay down at full length, for, if he had kept himself upright, his head would have reached too far above the clouds. Our philosophers then planted a tall tree in a place which Dr. Swift[7] would have named without hesitation, but which I abstain from mentioning out of my great respect for the ladies. Then by means of a series of triangles joined together, they came to the conclusion that the object before them was in reality a young man whose length was one hundred and twenty thousand statute feet.

Thereupon Micromégas uttered these words:

"I see more clearly than ever that we should judge of nothing by its apparent importance. O God, Who hast bestowed intelligence upon things which seemed so despicable, the infinitely little is as much Thy concern as the infinitely great; and, if it is possible that there should be living things smaller than these, they may be endowed with minds superior even to those of the magnificent creatures whom I have seen in the sky, who with one foot could cover this globe upon which I have alighted."

One of the philosophers replied that he might with perfect confidence believe that there actually were intelligent beings much smaller than man. He related, not indeed all the fables that Virgil has told on the subject of bees, but the results of Swammerdam's discoveries, and Réaumur's dissections. Finally, he informed him that there are animals which bear the same proportion to bees that bees bear to men, or that the Sirian himself bore to those huge creatures of which he spoke, or that those great creatures themselves bore to others before whom they seemed mere atoms. The conversation grew more and more interesting, and Micromégas spoke as follows.

Chapter 7

The Conversation Continued

"O INTELLIGENT ATOMS, in whom the eternal Being has been pleased to make manifest His skill and power, you must doubtless taste joys of perfect purity on this, your globe; for, being encumbered with so little matter, and seeming to be all spirit, you must pass your lives in love and meditation, which is the true life of spiritual beings. I have nowhere beheld genuine happiness, but here it is to be found without a doubt."

On hearing these words, all the philosophers shook their heads, and one of them, more frank than the others, candidly confessed that, with the exception of a small number held in little esteem among them, all the rest of mankind were a multitude of fools, knaves, and miserable wretches.

"We have more matter than we need," said he, "the cause of much evil, if evil proceeds from matter; and we have too much mind, if evil proceeds from the mind. Are you aware, for instance, that at this very moment while I am speaking to you, there are a hundred thousand fools of our species who wear hats, slaying a hundred thousand fellow creatures who wear turbans, or who are being massacred by them, and that over almost all the earth, such practices have been going on from time immemorial?"

The Sirian shuddered, and asked what could be the cause of such horrible quarrels between those miserable little creatures.

"The dispute is all about a lump of clay," said the philosopher, "no bigger than your heel. Not that a single one of those millions of men who get their throats cut has the slightest interest in this clod of earth. The only point in question is whether it shall belong to a certain man who is called Sultan, or to another who, I know not why, is called Cæsar. Neither the one nor the other has ever seen, or is ever likely to see, the little corner of ground which is the bone of contention; and hardly one of those animals, who are cutting each other's throats, has ever seen the animal for whom they fight so desperately."

"Ah, wretched creatures!" exclaimed the Sirian with indignation; "can anyone imagine such frantic ferocity! I should like to take two or three steps, and stamp upon the whole swarm of these ridiculous assassins."

"Do not give yourself the trouble," answered the philosopher; "they are working hard enough to destroy themselves. I assure you that at the end of ten years, not a hundredth part of those wretches will be left; even if they had never drawn the sword, famine, fatigue, or intemperance will sweep them almost all away. Besides, it is not they who deserve punishment, but rather those armchair barbarians, who from the privacy of their cabinets, and during the process of digestion, command the massacre of a million men, and afterwards ordain a solemn thanksgiving to God."

The traveler, moved with compassion for the tiny human race, among whom he found such astonishing contrasts, said to the gentlemen who were present:

"Since you belong to the small number of wise men, and apparently do not kill anyone for money, tell me, pray, how you occupy yourselves."

"We dissect flies," said the same philosopher, "we measure distances, we calculate numbers, we are agreed upon two or three points which we understand, and we dispute about two or three thousand as to which we know nothing."

The visitors from Sirius and Saturn were immediately seized with a desire to question these intelligent atoms on the subjects whereon their opinions coincided.

"How far do you reckon it," said the latter, "from the Dog-star to the great star in Gemini?"

They all answered together: "Thirty-two degrees and a half."

"How far do you make it from here to the moon?"

"Sixty half diameters of the earth, in round numbers."

"What is the weight of your air?"

He thought to lay a trap for them, but they all told him that the air weighs about nine hundred times less than an equal volume of distilled water, and nineteen thousand times less than pure gold.

The little dwarf from Saturn, astonished at their replies, was now inclined to take for sorcerers the same people to whom he had refused, a quarter of an hour ago, to allow the possession of a soul.

Then Micromégas said:

"Since you know so well what is outside of yourselves, doubtless you know still better what is within you. Tell me what is the nature of your soul, and how you form ideas."

The philosophers spoke all at once as before, but this time they were all of different opinions. The oldest of them quoted Aristotle, another pronounced the name of Descartes, this spoke of Malebranche, that of Leibnitz, and another again of Locke. The old Peripatetic said in a loud and confident tone of voice:

"The soul is an actuality and a rationality, in virtue of which it has the power to be what it is; as Aristotle expressly declares on page six hundred thirty-three of the Louvre edition of his works;" and he quoted the passage.

"I don't understand Greek very well," said the giant.

"No more do I," said the mite of a philosopher.

"Why, then," inquired the Sirian, "do you quote the man you call Aristotle in that language?"

"Because," replied the sage, "it is right and proper to quote what we do not comprehend at all in a language we least understand."

The Cartesian then interposed and said:

"The soul is pure spirit, which has received in its mother's womb all metaphysical ideas, and which, on issuing thence, is obliged to go to school, as it were, and learn afresh all that it knew so well, and which it will never know any more."

"It was hardly worth while, then," answered the eight-leagued giant, "for your soul to have been so learned in your mother's womb, if you were to become so ignorant by the time you have a beard on your chin.—But what do you understand by spirit?"

"Why do you ask me that question?" said the philosopher; "I have no idea of its meaning, except that it is said to be independent of matter."

"You know, at least, what matter is, I presume?"

"Perfectly well," replied the man. "For instance, this stone is gray, is of such and such a form, has three dimensions, has weight and divisibility."

"Very well," said the Sirian. "Now tell me, please, what this thing actually is which appears to you to be divisible, heavy, and of a gray color. You observe certain qualities, but are you acquainted with the intrinsic nature of the thing itself?"

"No," said the other.

"Then you do not know what matter is."

Thereupon Mr. Micromégas, addressing his question to another sage, whom he held on his thumb, asked him what the soul was, and what it did.

"Nothing at all," said the disciple of Malebranche; "it is God who does everything for me; I see and do everything through Him; He it is who does all without my interference."

"You might just as well, then, have no existence," replied the sage of Sirius.

"And you, my friend," he said to a follower of Leibnitz, who was there, "what is your soul?"

"It is," answered he, "a hand which points to the hour while my body chimes, or, if you like, it is the soul which chimes, while my body points to the hour; or, to put it in another way, my soul is the mirror of the universe, and my body is its frame: that is all clear enough."

A little student of Locke was standing near, and when his opinion at last was asked, he said:

"I know nothing of how I think, but I know that I have never thought except on the suggestion of my senses. That there are immaterial and intelligent substances is not what I doubt; but that it is impossible for God to communicate the faculty of thought to matter is what I doubt very strongly. I adore the eternal Power, nor is it my part to limit its exercise; I assert nothing, I content myself with believing that more is possible than people think."

The creature of Sirius smiled. He did not deem the last speaker the least sagacious of the company, and the dwarf of Saturn would have clasped Locke's disciple in his arms if their extreme disproportion had not made that impossible. But unluckily a little animalcule was there in a square cap,[8] who silenced all the other philosophical mites, saying that he knew the whole secret, that it was all to be found in the *Summa* of St. Thomas Aquinas; he scanned the pair of celestial visitors from top to toe, and maintained that they and all their kind, their suns and stars, were made solely for man's benefit. At this speech our two travelers tumbled over each other, choking with that inextinguishable laughter which, according to Homer, is the special privilege of the gods. Their shoulders shook, and their bodies heaved up and down, till, in those merry convulsions, the ship which the Sirian held on his nail fell into the Saturnian's breeches pocket. These two good people, after a long search, recovered it at last, and duly set to rights all that had been displaced. The Sirian once more took up the little mites, and addressed them again with great kindness, though he was a little disgusted in the bottom of his heart at seeing such infinitely insignificant atoms puffed up with a pride of such infinite magnitude. He promised to supply them with a rare book of philosophy, written in very minute characters for their special use, telling them that in that book they would find all that can be known of the ultimate essence of things, and he actually gave them the volume ere his departure. It was carried to Paris and laid before the Academy of Sciences; but when the old secretary came to open it, he saw nothing but blank leaves.

"Ah!" said he, "this is just what I expected."

JEANNOT AND COLIN

MANY TRUSTWORTHY PERSONS have seen Jeannot and Colin when they went to school at Issoire in Auvergne, a town famous all over the world for its college and its kettles. Jeannot was the son of a dealer in mules, a man of considerable reputation; Colin owed his existence to a worthy husbandman who dwelt in the outskirts of the town and cultivated his farm with the help of four mules, and who, after paying tolls and tallage, scutage and salt duty, poundage, poll-tax, and tithes, did not find himself particularly well off at the end of the year.

Jeannot and Colin were very handsome lads for natives of Auvergne; they were much attached to each other, and had little secrets together and private understandings, such as old comrades always recall with pleasure when they afterwards meet in a wider world.

Their school days were drawing near their end, when a tailor one day brought Jeannot a velvet coat of three colors with a waistcoat of Lyons silk to match in excellent taste; this suit of clothes was accompanied by a letter addressed to Monsieur de La Jeannotière. Colin admired the coat, and was not at all jealous, but Jeannot assumed an air of superiority which distressed Colin. From that moment Jeannot paid no more heed to his lessons, but was always looking at his reflection in the glass, and despised everybody but himself. Some time afterwards a footman arrived post-haste, bringing a second letter, addressed this time to His Lordship the Marquis de La Jeannotière; it contained an order from his father for the young nobleman, his son, to be sent to Paris. As Jeannot mounted the chaise to drive off, he stretched out his hand to Colin with a patronizing smile befitting his rank. Colin felt his own insignificance, and wept. So Jeannot departed in all his glory.

Readers who like to know all about things may be informed that Monsieur Jeannot, the father, had rapidly gained immense wealth in business. You ask how those great fortunes are made? It all depends upon luck. Monsieur Jeannotière had a comely person, and so had his wife; moreover her complexion was fresh and blooming. They had gone to Paris to prosecute a lawsuit which was ruining them, when Fortune, who lifts up and casts down human beings at her pleasure, presented them with an introduction to the wife of an army hospital contractor, a man of great talent, who could boast of having killed more soldiers in one year than the cannon had destroyed in ten. Jeannot took the lady's fancy, and Jeannot's wife captivated the gentleman. Jeannot soon became a partner in the business, and entered into other speculations. When one is in the current of the stream it is only necessary to let one's self drift, and so an immense fortune may sometimes be made without any trouble. The beggars who watch you from the bank, as you glide along in full sail, open their eyes in astonishment; they wonder how you have managed to get on; they envy you at all events, and write pamphlets against you which you never read. That was what happened to Jeannot senior, who was soon styled Monsieur de La Jeannotière, and, after buying a marquisate at the end of six months, he took the young nobleman, his son, away from school, to launch him into the fashionable world of Paris.

Colin, always affectionately disposed, wrote a kind letter to his old schoolfellow in order to offer his congratulations. The little marquis sent him no answer, which grieved Colin sorely.

The first thing that his father and mother did for the young gentleman was to get him a tutor. This tutor, who was a man of distinguished manners and profound ignorance, could teach his pupil nothing. The marquis wished his son to learn Latin, but the marchioness would not hear of it. They consulted the opinion of a certain author who had obtained considerable celebrity at that time from some popular works which he had written. He was invited to dinner, and the master of the house began by saying:

"Sir, as you know Latin, and are conversant with the manners of the Court—"

"I, sir! Latin! I don't know a word of it," answered the man of wit; "and it is just as well for me that I don't, for one can speak one's own language better, when the attention is not divided between it and foreign tongues. Look at all our ladies; they are far more charming in conversation than men, their letters are written with a hundred times more grace of expression. They owe that superiority over us to nothing else but their ignorance of Latin."

"There now! Was I not right?" said the lady. "I want my son to be a man of wit, and to make his way in the world. You see that if he were to learn Latin, it would be his ruin. Tell me, if you please, are plays and operas performed in Latin? Are the proceedings in court conducted in Latin when one has a lawsuit on hand? Do people make love in Latin?"

The marquis, confounded by these arguments, passed sentence, and it was decided that the young nobleman should not waste his time in studying Cicero, Horace, and Virgil.

"But what is he to learn then? For still, I suppose, he will have to know something. Might he not be taught a little geography?"

"What good will that do him?" answered the tutor. "When my lord marquis goes to visit his country seat, will not his postillions know the roads? There will be no fear of their going astray. One does not want a sextant in order to travel, and it is quite possible to make a journey from Paris to Auvergne without knowing anything about the latitude and longitude of either."

"Very true," replied the father. "But I have heard people speak of a noble science, which is, I think, called *astronomy*."

"Bless my soul!" rejoined the tutor. "Do we regulate our behavior in this world by the stars? Why should my lord marquis wear himself out in calculating an eclipse, when he will find it predicted correctly to a second in the almanac, which will, moreover, inform him of all the movable feasts, the age of the moon, and that of all the princesses in Europe?"

The marchioness was quite of the tutor's opinion, the little marquis was in a state of the highest delight, and his father was very undecided.

"What then is my son to be taught?" said he.

"To make himself agreeable," answered the friend whom they had consulted. "For, if he knows the way to please, he will know everything worth knowing; it is an art which he will learn from her ladyship, his mother, without the least trouble to either of them."

The marchioness, at these words, smiled graciously upon the courtly ignoramus, and said:

"It is easy to see, sir, that you are a most accomplished gentleman; my son will owe all his education to you. I imagine, however, that it will not be a bad thing for him to know a little history."

"Nay, madam,—what good would that do him?" he answered. "Assuredly the only entertaining and useful history is that of the passing hour. All ancient histories, as one of our clever writers[1] has observed, are admitted to be nothing but fables, and for us moderns it is an inextricable chaos. What does it matter to the young gentleman, your son, if Charlemagne instituted the twelve Paladins of France, or if his successor[2] had an impediment in his speech?"

"Nothing was ever said more wisely!" exclaimed the tutor. "The minds of children are smothered under a mass of useless knowledge, but of all sciences that which seems to me the most absurd, and the one best adapted to extinguish every spark of genius, is geometry. That ridiculous science is concerned with surfaces, lines, and points which have no existence in nature. In imagination a hundred thousand curved lines may be made to pass between a circle and a straight line which touches it, although in reality you could not insert so much as a straw. Geometry, indeed, is nothing more than a bad joke."

The marquis and his lady did not understand much of the meaning of what the tutor was saying; but they were quite of his way of thinking.

"A nobleman like his lordship," he continued, "should not dry up his brain with such unprofitable studies. If, some day, he should require one of those sublime geometricians to draw plans of his estates, he can have them measured for his money. If he should wish to trace out the antiquity of his lineage, which goes back to the most remote ages, all he will have to do will be to send for some learned Benedictine. It is the same with all the other arts. A young lord born under a lucky star is neither a painter, nor a musician, nor an architect, nor a sculptor; but he may make all these arts flourish by encouraging them with his generous approval. Doubtless it is much better to patronize them than to practice them. It will be quite enough if my lord the young marquis has taste; it is the part of artists to work for him, and thus there is a great deal of truth in the remark that people of quality (that is if they are very rich) know everything without learning anything, because, in point of fact and in the long run, they are masters of all the knowledge which they can command and pay for."

The agreeable ignoramus then took part again in the conversation, and said:

"You have well remarked, madam, that the great end of man's existence is to succeed in society. Is it, forsooth, any aid to the attainment of this success to have devoted one's self to the sciences? Does anyone ever think in select company of talking about geometry? Is a well-bred gentleman ever asked what star rises today with the sun? Does anyone at the supper table ever want to know if Clodion the Long Haired crossed the Rhine?"

"No, indeed!" exclaimed the Marchioness de La Jean-notière, whose charms had been her passport into the world of fashion; "and my son must not stifle his genius by studying all that rubbish. But, after all, what is he to be taught? For it is a good thing that a young lord should be able to shine when occasion offers, as my noble husband has said. I remember once hearing an abbé remark that the most entertaining science was something the name of which I have forgotten—it begins with a B."

"With a B, madam? It was not botany, was it?"

"No, it certainly was not botany that he mentioned; it began, as I tell you, with a B, and ended in *onry*."

"Ah, madam, I understand!—It was blazonry or heraldry. That is indeed a most profound science; but it has ceased to be fashionable since the custom has died out of having one's coat of arms painted on the carriage door, although it was the most useful thing imaginable in a well-ordered State. Besides, that line of study would be endless, for at the present day there is not a barber who is without his armorial bearings, and you know that whatever becomes common loses its attraction."

Finally, after all the pros and cons of the different sciences had been examined and discussed, it was decided that the young marquis should learn dancing.

Dame Nature, who disposes everything at her own will and pleasure, had given him a talent which soon developed itself with prodigious success: it was that of singing street ballads in a charming style. The youthful grace accompanying his superlative gift caused him to be regarded as a young man of the highest promise. He was a favorite with the ladies, and, having his head crammed with songs, he had no lack of mistresses to whom to address his verses. He stole the line "Bacchus with the Loves at play" from one ballad, and made it rhyme with "night and day" taken out of another, while a third furnished him with "charms" and "alarms." But inasmuch as there were always some feet more or less than were wanted in his verses, he had them corrected at the rate of twenty sovereigns a song. And *The Literary Year* placed him in the same rank with such sonneteers as La Fare, Chaulieu, Hamilton, Sarrasin, and Voiture.

Her ladyship the marchioness then believed that she was indeed the mother of a genius, and gave a supper to all the wits of Paris. The young man's head was soon turned upside down, he acquired the art of talking without knowing the meaning of what he said, and perfected himself in the habit of being fit for nothing. When his father saw him so eloquent, he keenly regretted that he had not had him taught Latin, or he would have purchased some high appointment for him in the Law. His mother, who was of more heroic sentiments, took upon herself to solicit a regiment for her son. In the meantime he made love,—and love is sometimes more expensive than a regiment. He squandered his money freely, while his parents drained their purses and credit to a lower and lower ebb by living in the grandest style.

A young widow of good position in their neighborhood, who had only a moderate income, was well enough disposed to make some effort to prevent the great wealth of the Marquis and Marchioness de La Jeannotière from going altogether, by marrying the young marquis and so appropriating what remained. She enticed him to her house, let him make love to her, allowed him to see that she was not quite indifferent to him, led him on by degrees, enchanted him, and made him her devoted slave without the least difficulty. She would give him at one time commendation and at another time counsel; she became his father's and mother's best friend. An old neighbor proposed marriage; the parents, dazzled with the splendor of the alliance, joyfully fell in with the scheme, and gave their only son to their most intimate lady friend. The young marquis was thus about to wed a woman whom he adored, and by whom he was beloved in return. The friends of the family congratulated him, the marriage settlement was on the point of being signed, the bridal dress and the epithalamium were both well under way.

One morning our young gentleman was on his knees before the charmer whom fond affection and esteem were so soon to make his own; they were tasting in animated and tender converse the first fruits of future happiness; they were settling how they should lead a life of perfect bliss, when one of his lady mother's footmen presented himself, scared out of his wits.

"Here's fine news which may surprise you!" said he. "The bailiffs are in the house of my lord and lady, removing the furniture. All has been seized by the creditors. They talk of personal arrests, and I am going to do what I can to get my wages paid."

"Let us see what has happened," said the marquis, "and discover the meaning of all this."

"Yes," said the widow, "go and punish those rascals —go, quick!"

He hurried homewards, he arrived at the house; his father was already in prison, all the servants had fled, each in a different direction, carrying off whatever they could lay their hands upon. His mother was alone, helpless, forlorn, and bathed in tears; she had nothing left her but the remembrance of her former prosperity, her beauty, her faults, and her foolish extravagance.

After the son had condoled with his mother for a long time, he said at last:

"Let us not despair; this young widow loves me to distraction; she is even more generous than she is wealthy, I can assure you, I will fly to her for succor, and bring her to you."

So he returns to his mistress, and finds her conversing in private with a fascinating young officer.

"What! Is that you, my lord de La Jeannotière? What business have you with me? How can you leave your mother by herself in this way? Go, and stay with the poor woman, and tell her that she shall always have my good wishes. I am in want of a waiting-woman now, and will gladly give her the preference."

"My lad," said the officer, "you seem pretty tall and straight; if you would like to enter my company, I will make it worth your while to enlist."

The marquis, stupefied with astonishment, and secretly enraged, went off in search of his former tutor, confided to him all his troubles, and asked his advice. He proposed that he should become, like himself, a tutor of the young.

"Alas! I know nothing; you have taught me nothing whatever, and you are the primary cause of all my unhappiness." And as he spoke he began to sob.

"Write novels," said a wit who was present; "it is an excellent resource to fall back upon at Paris."

The young man, in more desperate straits than ever, hastened to the house of his mother's father-confessor, who was a Theatine monk of the very highest reputation, directing the souls of none but ladies of the first rank in society. As soon as he saw him, the reverend gentleman rushed to meet him.

"Good gracious! My lord Marquis, where is your carriage? How is your honored mother, the Marchioness?"

The unfortunate young fellow related the disaster that had befallen his family. As he explained the matter further the Theatine[3] assumed a graver air, one of less concern and more self-importance.

"My son, herein you may see the hand of Providence; riches serve only to corrupt the heart. The Almighty has shown special favor then to your mother in reducing her to beggary. Yes, sir, so much the better!—She is now sure of her salvation."

"But, father, in the meantime are there no means of obtaining some succor in this world?"

"Farewell, my son! There is a lady of the Court waiting for me."

The marquis felt ready to faint. He was treated after much the same manner by all his friends, and learned to know the world better in half a day than in all the rest of his life.

As he was plunged in overwhelming despair, he saw an old-fashioned traveling chaise, more like a covered tumbril than anything else and furnished with leather curtains, followed by four enormous wagons all heavily laden. In the chaise was a young man in rustic attire; his round and rubicund face had an air of kindness and good temper. His little wife, whose sunburned countenance had a pleasing if not a refined expression, was jolted about as she sat beside him. The vehicle did not go quite so fast as a dandy's chariot, the traveler had plenty of time to look at the marquis, as he stood motionless, absorbed in his grief.

"Oh, good heavens!" he exclaimed; "I believe that is Jeannot there!"

Hearing that name the marquis raised his eyes; the chaise stopped.

"'Tis Jeannot himself! Yes, it is Jeannot!"

The plump little man with one leap sprang to the ground, and ran to embrace his old companion. Jeannot recognized Colin; signs of sorrow and shame covered his countenance.

"You have forsaken your old friend," said Colin, "but be you as grand a lord as you like, I shall never cease to love you."

Jeannot, confounded and cut to the heart, told him with sobs something of his history.

"Come into the inn where I am lodging, and tell me the rest," said Colin; "kiss my little wife, and let us go and dine together."

They went, all three of them, on foot, and the baggage followed.

"What in the world is all this paraphernalia? Does it belong to you?"

"Yes, it is all mine and my wife's, we are just come from the country. I am at the head of a large tin, iron, and copper factory, and have married the daughter of a rich tradesman and general provider of all useful commodities for great folks and small. We work hard, and God gives us his blessing. We are satisfied with our condition in life, and are quite happy. We will help our friend Jeannot! Give up being a marquis; all the grandeur in the world is not equal in value to a good friend. You will return with me into the country; I will teach you my trade, it is not a difficult one to learn; I will give you a share in the business, and we will live together with light hearts in that corner of the earth where we were born."

Jeannot, overcome by this kindness, felt himself divided between sorrow and joy, tenderness and shame, and he said to himself:

"All my fashionable friends have proved false to me, and Colin, whom I despised, is the only one who comes to my succor. What a lesson!"

Colin's generosity developed in Jeannot's heart the germ of that good disposition which the world had not yet choked. He felt that he could not desert his father and mother.

"We will take care of your mother," said Colin; "and as for your good father, who is in prison,—I know something of business matters,—his creditors, when they see that he has nothing more, will agree to a moderate compensation. I will see to all that myself."

Colin was as good as his word, and succeeded in effecting the father's release from prison. Jeannot returned to his old home with his parents, who resumed their former occupation. He married Colin's sister, who, being like her brother in disposition, rendered her husband very happy. And so Jeannot the father, and Jeannotte the mother, and Jeannot the son came to see that vanity is no true source of happiness.

THE STORY OF A GOOD BRAHMAN

I ONCE MET, when on my travels, an old Brahman who was exceedingly wise, full of native intelligence, and profoundly learned. Moreover, he was rich, and, in consequence, all the more correct in his conduct, for, being in want of nothing, he had no need to deceive anybody. His household was very well managed by three handsome wives who laid themselves out to please him; and, when he was not entertaining himself with them, he was engaged in studying philosophy.

Near his house, which was a fine one situated in the midst of charming gardens, dwelt an old Hindoo woman, bigoted, half-witted, and extremely poor.

One day the Brahman said to me:

"Would that I had never been born!"

I asked him what made him say that, and he replied as follows:

"I studied for forty years, and they are so many years wasted; I have been teaching for the rest of my life, and I am ignorant of everything. This state of things fills my soul with such humiliation and disgust, that life is to me intolerable. I have been born into the world, I live subject to the limitations of time, and I know not what time is: I find myself on a point between two eternities, as our sages say, and I have no conception of eternity. I am composed of matter, and I can think, yet I have never been able to satisfy myself as to what produces thought: I know not whether my understanding is a simple faculty within me, like the power of walking or of digesting food, and whether I think with my head in the same way as I grasp with my hands. Not only is the essential nature of my powers of thought unknown to me, but that of my muscular movements is equally obscure. I cannot tell why I exist, yet I am questioned every day on all these points, and I am obliged to make some answer. I have nothing to say worth hearing, but I am not sparing of my words, and, after all has been said, I remain confused and ashamed of myself.

"It is even worse when people ask me if Brahma was produced by Vishnu, or if they are both eternal. Heaven is my witness that I know nothing about the matter, as my answers only too plainly show. 'Ah, reverend father,' they say, 'teach us how it is that evil floods the whole earth!' I am as much at a loss as those who ask me that question; I tell them sometimes that all is well and could not be better, but those who have been ruined and maimed in the wars do not believe a word of it, any more than I do myself. I retire into my own house crushed by the weight of my own ignorance and unsatisfied curiosity. I read our ancient books, and they only make my darkness greater. I speak to my companions; some tell me in reply that we must enjoy life and laugh at mankind, others think that they know a secret that explains everything, and lose themselves in a maze of extravagant notions. All tends to increase the painful feeling of uncertainty that possesses me, and I am ready sometimes to fall into despair, when I consider that, after all my investigations, I know neither whence I come, nor what I am, nor whither I go, nor what will become of me."

I was really pained at the state of this good soul; no one could be more rational than he was, nor more sincerely in earnest. I conceived that the brighter the light of his understanding, and the keener the sensibility of his heart, the greater was his unhappiness.

The same day I saw the old woman who lived in his neighborhood, and I asked her if she had ever been distressed at not knowing how her soul was formed. She did not even comprehend my question; she had never reflected for a single moment of her life on any one of those points which tormented the Brahman; she believed in the incarnation of Vishnu with all her heart, and provided she might sometimes have a little water from the Ganges with which to wash herself, she deemed herself the most fortunate of women.

Struck with this poor creature's happiness, I returned to my philosopher, and said:

"Are you not ashamed of being unhappy, while at your very gate there is an old automaton who thinks about nothing and lives contented?"

"You are right," he answered; "I have told myself a hundred times that I should be happy if I were as silly as my neighbor, and yet somehow I have no wish to attain such happiness."

This reply of my Brahman impressed me more than anything else. I examined my own heart and discovered that, if I had the offer, I should not have wished, any more than he, to be happy at the expense of my intelligence.

I referred the problem to some philosophers, and their opinions were the same as mine.

"For all that," said I, "There is a wild contradiction in this manner of thinking; for, after all, what is the question?—How to be happy. What does it matter whether one is intelligent or silly? Moreover, those who are contented with their existence are quite sure that they are so, whereas those who exercise their reason are by no means so certain that they exercise it aright. It is clear then," said I, "that we should be constrained to choose the loss of reason, if reason contributes to our unhappiness in however small a degree."

Everybody agreed with me in this opinion, and yet I found no one willing to accept the bargain, when it was a question of purchasing contentment at the price of becoming a fool. Hence I concluded that if we set a high value on happiness, we value reason even more.

But, after having reflected on this matter, it appears to me that to prefer reason to happiness is to be very senseless. How can this contradiction be explained? Like all the others—whereon there is a great deal to be said.

MEMNON, THE PHILOSOPHER

Notice by the Author

In all we undertake we miss the way:
    That is, alas! our destined fate, it seems.
    My brain at morn with wisest projects teems,
While folly chases folly all the day.

THIS LITTLE VERSE pretty aptly describes a large number of those who pride themselves on the possession of reason, and it is odd enough to see a grave director of souls ending his career in the criminal dock beside a fraudulent bankrupt. In connection with this case, we reprint here the following little tale, though it had its origin elsewhere, for it is well that it should be known far and wide.

Memnon one day conceived the irrational design of being perfectly wise and prudent. There are very few persons who have not at some time or other had foolish thoughts of this kind pass through their heads. Memnon said to himself: "In order to be very wise, and consequently very happy, one has only to be without passions, and nothing is easier than that, as everybody knows. In the first place, I will never fall in love with a woman, for I will say to myself, whenever I see a sample of perfect beauty: 'Those cheeks will one day be wrinkled, those fine eyes will be rimmed with red, that swelling bosom will be flat and flabby, that lovely head will become bald.' I have only to see her now with the same eyes as those with which I shall see her then, and assuredly my head will not be turned by the sight of hers.

"In the second place, I will be always sober and temperate; good cheer, delicious wines, and the seductive charms of social intercourse will tempt me in vain. I shall have nothing to do but to bring before my mind the results of excess in a heavy head, a disordered stomach, the loss of reason, of health, and of time, and then I shall eat only for necessity, my health will be always well balanced, my thoughts always bright and clear. All this is so easy that there is no merit in such attainments.

"In the next place," said Memnon, "I must give a little consideration to my property; my desires are moderate, my wealth is well bestowed with the receiver-general of the revenues of Nineveh, I have enough to support myself in independence, and that is the greatest of blessings. I shall never be under the cruel necessity of cringing and flattering; I shall envy nobody, and nobody will envy me. All that is still very easy. I have friends," continued he, "and I shall keep them, for they will have nothing to quarrel about with me. I will never be out of temper with them, nor they with me; that is a matter that presents no difficulty."

Having thus laid down his little scheme of wisdom and prudence in his chamber, Memnon put his head out of the window, and saw two women walking up and down under some plane trees near his house. One of them was old, and appeared to have nothing on her mind; the other was young and pretty, and seemed to be lost in thought. She sighed, she wept, and her sighs and tears only added to her charms. Our sage was touched, not, of course, by the lady's beauty (he was quite confident of being above such weakness as that), but by the distress in which he saw her. He went down and accosted the fair Ninevite, with the intention of ministering wise consolation. That charming young person related to him, with the most simple and affecting air, all the injury done her by an uncle, who did not exist; she told him by what tricks he had deprived her of a fortune, which she had never possessed, and all that she had to fear from his violence.

"You seem to me," said she, "a man of such excellent judgment and good sense, that if you would only condescend to come to my house and inquire into my affairs, I feel sure that you could extricate me from the cruel embarrassment in which I find myself."

Memnon had no hesitation in following her, in order to make a judicious examination of her affairs, and to give her good advice.

The afflicted lady led him into a sweetly-scented chamber, and politely made him sit down with her on a large ottoman, where they both remained awhile, with legs crossed, facing each other. When the lady spoke she lowered her eyes, from which tears sometimes escaped, and, when she raised them, they always met the gaze of the sage Memnon. Her language was full of a tenderness which grew more tender each time that they exchanged glances. Memnon took her affairs zealously to heart, and every moment felt an increasing desire to oblige a maiden so modest and so unfortunate. By imperceptible degrees, as their conversation grew warmer, they ceased to sit opposite each other, and their legs were no longer crossed. Memnon pressed her so closely with good advice, and bestowed such tender admonitions, that neither of them could any longer talk about business, nor did they well know what they were about.

While they were thus engaged, the uncle, as might have been expected, arrived upon the scene. He was armed from head to foot, and the first thing he said was that he was going to kill, as was only just and proper, both the sage Memnon and his niece. The last remark that escaped him was that he might possibly pardon them for a large sum of money. Memnon was obliged to give him all that he had about him. In those times, fortunately, it was possible to get off as cheaply as that. America had not yet been discovered, and distressed damsels were not nearly so dangerous as they are nowadays.

Memnon returned home disconsolate and ashamed, and found a note there inviting him to dine with some of his most intimate friends.

"If I stay at home alone," said he, "I shall have my thoughts taken up with my unfortunate adventure, I shall be unable to eat anything, and shall certainly fall ill; it will be much better to take a frugal meal with my intimate friends. In the pleasure of their company I shall forget the piece of folly that I have committed this morning."

He goes to meet his friends, who find him a little out of spirits, and persuade him to drink away his melancholy. A little wine taken in moderation is a medicine for mind and body. So thinks the sage Memnon, and proceeds to get tipsy. Play is proposed after dinner. A modest game with one's friends is a blameless pastime. He plays, loses all that he has in his purse, and four times as much on his promise to pay. A dispute arises over the game, and the quarrel grows hot; one of his intimate friends throws a dice box at his head, and puts out an eye. The sage Memnon is carried home drunk, without any money, and with one eye less than when he went.

After he had slept himself sober, and his brain was grown a little clearer, he sent his servant for some of the money which he had lodged with the receiver-general of the revenues of Nineveh, in order to pay what he owed to his intimate friends. He was told that his debtor had that very morning been declared a fraudulent bankrupt, an announcement which had thrown a hundred families into consternation. Memnon, in a state bordering on distraction, went to court with a plaster over his eye and a petition in his hand to solicit justice of the king against the bankrupt. In an antechamber he met a number of ladies, all wearing with apparent ease hoops twenty-four feet in circumference. One of these ladies, who knew him slightly, exclaimed with a sidelong glance: "Oh, what a horror!" Another, who was on more familiar terms with him, addressed him thus:

"Good evening, Mr. Memnon. It is indeed a pleasure to see you, Mr. Memnon. By the way, Mr. Memnon, how is it you have lost an eye?" And she passed on without pausing for an answer. Memnon hid himself in a corner, and awaited the moment when he might cast himself at the monarch's feet. That moment came; he kissed the ground thrice, and presented his petition. His Gracious Majesty received him very favorably, and gave the document to one of his satraps to report upon it. The satrap drew Memnon aside, and said:

"What a comical kind of one-eyed fool you are, to address yourself to the king rather than to me! And still more ridiculous to dare to demand justice against a respectable bankrupt, whom I honor with my protection, and who is the nephew of my mistress's waiting-maid. Let this matter drop, my friend, if you wish to keep the eye you still have left you."

Thus Memnon, after having in the morning renounced the blandishments of women, intemperance at table, gambling and quarreling, and more than all else the court, had ere nightfall been cajoled and robbed by a fair deceiver, had drunk to excess, played high, been concerned in a quarrel, had an eye put out, and been to court, where he had been treated with contempt and derision.

Petrified with astonishment, and crushed with vexation, he turned his steps homeward, sick at heart. Intending to enter his house, he found bailiffs in possession removing the furniture on behalf of his creditors. Almost fainting, he seated himself under a plane tree, and there encountered the fair lady who had victimized him in the morning. She was walking with her dear uncle, and burst out laughing when she saw Memnon with the patch over his eye. Night came on; and Memnon laid himself down on some straw beside the walls of his house. There he was seized with ague, and in one of the fits he fell asleep, when a celestial spirit appeared to him in a dream.

He was all glittering with light. He had six beautiful wings, but no feet, nor head, nor tail, and was like nothing he had ever seen before.

"Who art thou?" said Memnon.

"Thy good genius," answered the other.

"Give me back my eye then, my health, my house, my property, and my prudence," said Memnon. Thereupon he told him how he had lost them all in one day.

"Such adventures as those never befall us in the world which we inhabit," said the spirit.

"And what world do you inhabit?" asked the afflicted mortal.

"My home," replied he, "is at a distance of five hundred millions of leagues from the sun, in a little star near Sirius, which thou seest from hence."

"Charming country!" exclaimed Memnon. "What! Have you no sly hussies among you who impose upon a poor fellow, no intimate friends who win his money and knock out one of his eyes, no bankrupts, no satraps who mock you while they deny you justice?"

"No," said the inhabitant of the star, "nothing of the kind. We are never deceived by women, because we have none; we are never guilty of excesses at table, since we neither eat nor drink; we have no bankrupts, for gold and silver are unknown among us; we cannot have our eyes put out, because we do not possess bodies such as yours; and satraps never treat us with injustice, since all are equal in our little star."

Then said Memnon: "My lord, without the fair sex and without any dinner, how do you manage to pass the time?"

"In watching over the other worlds which are intrusted to our care," said the genius; "and I am come now to minister consolation to thee."

"Alas!" replied Memnon, "why didst thou not come last night to prevent me committing such follies?"

"I was with Hassan, your elder brother," said the celestial being. "He is more to be pitied than thou art. His Gracious Majesty, the King of India, to whose court he has the honor to be attached, has caused both his eyes to be put out for a slight act of indiscretion, and he is confined at the present moment in a dungeon, with chains upon his hands and feet."

"It is indeed well worth while to have a good genius in a family!" said Memnon; "of two brothers one has an eye knocked out, and the other loses both, one lies on straw, the other in prison."

"Thy lot will change," answered the inhabitant of the star. "It is true that thou wilt never recover thine eye, but, for all that, thou wilt be tolerably happy, provided that thou does never entertain the foolish idea of being perfectly wise and prudent."

"Is it impossible then to attain such a condition?" cried Memnon with a sigh.

"As impossible," replied the other, "as to be perfectly clever, perfectly strong, perfectly powerful, or perfectly happy. Even we ourselves are very far from being so. There is indeed a sphere where all that is to be found, but in the hundred thousand millions of worlds which are scattered through space everything proceeds by degrees. There is less wisdom and enjoyment in the second than in the first, less in the third than in the second, and so on to the last, where everybody is an absolute fool."

"I very much fear," said Memnon, "that our little terraqueous globe is precisely that lunatic asylum of the universe of which thou dost me the honor to speak."

"Not quite," said the spirit; "but it is not far off; everything must occupy its own place."

"In that case," said Memnon, "certain poets and certain philosophers are much mistaken when they say that *everything is for the best*, is it not so?"

"They are quite right," said the philosopher from the world above, "when the arrangement of the whole universe is taken into consideration."

"Ah! I shall never believe that," answered poor Memnon, "till I see out of two eyes again."

THE WORLD IS LIKE THAT, OR
THE VISION OF BABOUC

Chapter 1

AMONG THE GENII who preside over the empires of the world, Ithuriel holds one of the first places, and has the province of Upper Asia. He came down one morning, entered the dwelling of Babouc, a Scythian who lived on the banks of the Oxus, and addressed him thus:

"Babouc, the follies and disorders of the Persians have drawn down upon them our wrath. An assembly of the genii of Upper Asia was held yesterday to consider whether Persepolis should be punished or utterly destroyed. Go thither, and make full investigation; on thy return inform me faithfully of all, and I will decide according to thy report either to chastise the city or to root it out."

"But, my lord," said Babouc humbly, "I have never been in Persia, and know no one there."

"So much the better," said the angel, "thou wilt be the more impartial. Heaven has given thee discernment, and I add the gift of winning confidence. Go, look, listen, observe, and fear nothing; thou shalt be well received everywhere."

Babouc mounted his camel, and set out with his servants. After some days, on approaching the plains of Sennah, he fell in with the Persian army, which was going to fight with the army of India.[1] He first accosted a soldier whom he found at a distance from the camp, and asked him what was the cause of the war.

"By all the gods," said the soldier, "I know nothing about it; it is no business of mine, my trade is to kill and be killed to get a living. It makes no odds to me whom I serve. I have a great mind to pass over tomorrow into the Indian camp, for I fear that they are giving their men half a copper drachma a day more than we get in this cursed

service of Persia. If you want to know why we are fighting, speak to
my captain."

Babouc gave the soldier a small present, and entered the camp.
He soon made the captain's acquaintance, and asked him the cause
of the war.

"How should I know?" said he. "Such grand matters are no concern
of mine. I live two hundred leagues away from Persepolis; I hear it
said that war has been declared; I immediately forsake my family,
and go, according to our custom, to make my fortune or to die, since
I have nothing else to do."

"But surely," said Babouc, "your comrades are a little better
informed than yourself?"

"No," replied the officer, "hardly anybody except our chief satraps
has any very clear notion why we are cutting each other's throats."

Babouc, astonished at this, introduced himself to the generals, and
they were soon on intimate terms. At last one of them said to him:

"The cause of this war, which has laid Asia waste for the last twenty
years, originally sprang out of a quarrel between a eunuch belonging
to one of the wives of the great King of Persia, and a customhouse
clerk in the service of the great King of India. The matter in dispute
was a duty amounting to very nearly the thirtieth part of a daric.[2]
The Indian and Persian prime ministers worthily supported their
masters' rights. The quarrel grew hot. They sent into the field on
both sides an army of a million troops. This army has to be recruited
every year with more than 400,000 men. Massacres, conflagrations,
ruin, and devastation multiply, the whole world suffers, and their
fury still continues. Our own as well as the Indian prime minister
often protests that they are acting solely for the happiness of the
human race, and at each protestation some towns are always destroyed
and some province ravaged."

The next day, on a report being spread that peace was about to
be concluded, the Persian and Indian generals hastened to give battle;
and a bloody one it was. Babouc saw all its mistakes and all its
abominations: he witnessed stratagems carried on by the chief satraps,
who did all they could to cause their commander to be defeated; he
saw officers slain by their own troops; he saw soldiers dispatching
their dying comrades in order to strip them of a few blood-stained
rags, torn and covered with mud. He entered the hospitals to which
they were carrying the wounded, most of whom died through the
inhuman negligence of those very men whom the King of Persia
paid handsomely to relieve them.

"Are these creatures men," cried Babouc, "or wild beasts? Ah! I see plainly that Persepolis will be destroyed."

Occupied with this thought, he passed into the camp of the Indians, and found there as favorable a reception as in that of the Persians, just as he had been led to expect; but he beheld there all the same abuses that had already filled him with horror.

"Ah!" said he to himself, "if the angel Ithuriel resolves to exterminate the Persians, then the angel of India must destroy the Indians as well."

Being afterwards more particularly informed of all that went on in both camps, he was made acquainted with acts of generosity, magnanimity, and humanity that moved him with astonishment and delight.

"Unintelligible mortals!" he exclaimed, "how is it that ye can combine so much meanness with so much greatness, such virtues with such crimes?"

Meanwhile peace was declared. The commanders of both armies, neither of whom had gained the victory but who had caused the blood of so many of their fellow men to flow, only to promote their own interests, began to solicit rewards at their respective courts. The peace was extolled in public proclamations, which announced nothing less than the return of virtue and happiness to earth.

"God be praised!" said Babouc, "Persepolis will be the abode of purified innocence. It will not be destroyed, as those rascally genii wished: let us hasten without delay to this capital of Asia."

Chapter 2

ON HIS ARRIVAL he entered that immense city by the old approach, which was altogether barbarous and offended the eye with its hideous want of taste.[3] All that part of the city bore witness to the time at which it had been built, for, in spite of men's obstinate stupidity in praising ancient at the expense of modern times, it must be confessed that in every kind of art first attempts are always rude.

Babouc mingled in a crowd of people composed of all the dirtiest and ugliest of both sexes, who with a dull and sullen air were pouring into a vast and dreary building. From the constant hum of voices and the movements that he remarked, from the money that some were giving to others for the privilege of sitting down, he thought that he was in a market where straw-bottomed chairs were on sale. But soon, when he observed several women drop upon their knees, pretending to look fixedly before them, but giving sidelong glances at the men, he became aware that he was in a temple. Grating voices, harsh, disagreeable, and out of tune, made the roof echo with ill-articulated sounds, which produced much the same effect as the braying of wild asses on the plains of the Pictavians,[4] when they answer the summons of the cow-herd's horn. He shut his ears, but he was yet more anxious to shut his eyes and nose, when he saw workmen entering this temple with crowbars and spades, who removed a large stone, and threw up the earth to right and left, from which there issued a most offensive smell. Then people came and laid a dead body in the opening, and the stone was put back above it.

"What!" cried Babouc, "these folk bury their dead in the same places where they worship the Deity, and their temples are paved with corpses! I am no longer surprised at those pestilential diseases which often consume Persepolis. The air, tainted with the corruption of the dead and by so many of the living gathered and crammed together in the same place, is enough to poison the whole earth. Oh, what an abominable city is this Persepolis! It would seem that the angels intend to destroy it in order to raise up a fairer one on its site, and to fill it with cleaner inhabitants, and such as can sing better. Providence may be right after all; let us leave it to take its own course."

Chapter 3

MEANWHILE THE SUN had almost reached the middle of its course. Babouc was to dine at the other end of the town with a lady for whom he had letters from her husband, an officer in the army. He first took several turns in and about Persepolis, where he saw other temples better built and more tastefully adorned, filled with a refined congregation, and resounding with harmonious music. He observed public fountains, which, badly placed though they were, struck the eye by their beauty; open spaces, where the best kings who had governed Persia seemed to breathe in bronze, and others where he heard the people exclaiming: "When shall we see our beloved master here?" He admired the magnificent bridges that spanned the river, the splendid and serviceable quays, the palaces built on either side, and especially an immense mansion where thousands of old soldiers, wounded in the hour of victory, daily returned thanks to the God of armies.[5] At last he entered the lady's house, where he had been invited to dine with a select company. The rooms were elegant and handsomely furnished, the dinner delicious, the lady young, beautiful, clever and charming, the company worthy of their hostess, and Babouc kept saying to himself every moment: "The angel Ithuriel must set the opinion of the whole world at defiance, if he thinks of destroying a city so delightful."

Chapter 4

AS TIME WENT on he perceived that the lady, who had begun by making tender inquiries after her husband, was, towards the end of the repast, speaking more tenderly still to a young magian. He saw a magistrate who, in his wife's presence, was bestowing the liveliest caresses upon a widow; and that indulgent widow kept one hand round the magistrate's neck, while she stretched out the other to a handsome young citizen whose modesty seemed equal to his good looks. The magistrate's wife was the first to leave the table, in order to entertain in an adjoining chamber her spiritual director, who had been expected to dine with them but arrived too late; and the director, a man of ready eloquence, addressed her in that chamber with such vigor and unction, that the lady, when she came back, had her eyes moist and her cheeks flushed, an unsteady step, and a stammering utterance.

Then Babouc began to fear that the genius Ithuriel was in the right. The gift that he possessed of winning confidence let him into the secrets of his fair hostess that very day; she owned to him her partiality for the young magian, and assured him that in all the houses at Persepolis he would find the same sort of behavior as he had witnessed in hers. Babouc came to the conclusion that such a society could not long hold together; that jealousy, discord, and revenge were bound to make havoc in every household; that tears and blood must be shed daily; that the husbands would assuredly kill or be killed by the lovers of their wives; and, finally, that Ithuriel would do well to destroy immediately a city given up to continual dissensions.

Chapter 5

HE WAS BROODING over these doleful thoughts, when there appeared at the door a man of grave countenance, clad in a black cloak, who humbly entreated a word with the young magistrate. The latter, without getting up or even looking at him, gave him some papers with a haughty and absent air, and then dismissed him. Babouc asked who the man was. The mistress of the house said to him in a low tone:

"That is one of the ablest counselors we have in this city, and he has been studying the laws for fifty years. The gentleman yonder, who is but twenty-five years of age, and who was made a satrap of the law two days ago, has employed him to draw up an abstract of a case on which he has to pronounce judgment tomorrow, and which he has not yet examined."

"This young spark acts wisely," said Babouc, "in asking an old man's advice, but why is not that old man himself the judge?"

"You must be joking," was the reply; "those who have grown old in toilsome and inferior employments never attain positions of great dignity. This young man enjoys a high office because his father is rich, and because the right of administering justice is bought and sold here like a farm."

"O unhappy city, to have such customs!" cried Babouc. "That is the coping-stone of confusion. Doubtless those who have purchased the right of dispensing justice sell their judgments. I see nothing here but unfathomable depths of iniquity."

As he thus testified his sorrow and surprise, a young warrior, who had that very day returned from the campaign, addressed him in the following terms:

"Why should you object to judicial appointments being made a matter of purchase? I have myself paid a good price for the right of facing death at the head of two thousand men under my command; it has cost me forty thousand gold darics this year to lie on the bare ground in a red coat for thirty nights together and to be twice wounded pretty severely by an arrow, of which I still feel the smart. If I ruin myself to serve the Persian emperor whom I have never seen, this gentleman who represents the majesty of the law may well pay something to have the pleasure of listening to litigants."

Babouc in his indignation could not refrain from condemning in his heart a country where the highest offices of peace and war were put up to auction; he hastily concluded that there must be among such people a total ignorance of legal and military affairs, and that even if Ithuriel should spare them, they would be destroyed by their own detestable institutions.

His bad opinion was further confirmed by the arrival of a fat man, who, after giving a familiar nod to all the company, approached the young officer, and said to him:

"I can only lend you fifty thousand gold darics; for to tell you the truth, the imperial taxes have not brought me in more than three hundred thousand this year."

Babouc inquired who this man might be who complained of getting so little, and was informed that there were in Persepolis forty plebeian kings, who held the Persian empire on lease, and paid the monarch something out of what they made.

Chapter 6

AFTER DINNER HE went into one of the grandest temples in the city, and seated himself in the midst of a crowd of men and women who had come there to pass away the time. A magian appeared in a structure raised above their heads, and spoke for a long time about virtue and vice. This magian divided under several heads what had no need of division, he proved methodically what was perfectly clear, and taught what everybody knew already. He coolly worked himself into a passion, and went away perspiring and out of breath. Then all the congregation awoke, and thought that they had been listening to an edifying discourse. Babouc said:

"There is a man who has done his best to weary two or three hundred of his fellow citizens, but his intention was good, and there is no reason in that for destroying Persepolis."

On leaving this assembly, he was taken to witness a public entertainment, which was exhibited every day in the year. It was held in a sort of hall, at the further end of which appeared a palace. The fairest part of the female population of Persepolis and the most illustrious satraps, seated in orderly ranks, formed a spectacle so brilliant that Babouc imagined at first that there was nothing more to be seen. Two or three persons, who seemed to be kings and queens, soon showed themselves at the entrance of the palace; their language was very different from that of the people; it was measured, harmonious, and sublime. No one slept, but all listened in profound silence, which was only interrupted by expressions of feeling and admiration on the part of the audience. The duty of kings, the love of virtue, and the dangerous nature of the passions were set forth in terms so lively and touching that Babouc shed tears. He had no doubt that those heroes and heroines, those kings and queens, whom he had just heard, were the preachers of the empire. He even proposed to himself to persuade Ithuriel to come and hear them, quite convinced that such a spectacle would reconcile him forever to the city.

As soon as the entertainment was over, he was anxious to see the principal queen, who had delivered such pure and noble sentiments of morality in that beautiful palace. He procured an introduction to her majesty, and was led up a narrow staircase to the second story, and ushered into a badly furnished apartment, where he found a woman meanly clad, who said to him with a noble and pathetic air:

"This calling of mine does not afford me enough to live upon; one of the princes whom you saw has got me into the family way, and I shall soon be brought to bed. I am in want of money, and one cannot lie in without that."

Babouc gave her a hundred gold darics, saying to himself:

"If there were nothing worse than this in the city, I think Ithuriel would be wrong in being so angry."

After that he went, under the escort of an intelligent man with whom he had become acquainted, to pass the evening in the shops of those who dealt in objects of useless ostentation. He bought whatever took his fancy, and everything was sold him in the most polite manner at far more than it was worth. His friend, on their return to his house, explained to him how he had been cheated, and Babouc made a note of the tradesman's name, in order to have him specially marked out by Ithuriel on the day when the city should be visited with punishment. As he was writing, a knock was heard at the door; it was the shopkeeper himself come to restore his purse, which Babouc had left by mistake on his counter.

"How comes it to pass," cried Babouc, "that you can be so honest and generous, after having had the face to sell me a lot of trumpery for four times as much as it is worth?"

"There is no merchant of any note in this city," answered the shopkeeper, "who would not have brought you back your purse, but whoever told you that you paid four times its proper value for what you bought from me, has grossly deceived you. My profit was ten times as much, and so true is this that if you wish to sell the articles again in a month's time, you will not get even that tenth part. But nothing is fairer; it is men's passing fancy which settles the price of such gewgaws; it is that fancy which affords a livelihood to the hundred workmen whom I employ; it is that which provides me with a fine house, a comfortable carriage, and horses; it is that which stimulates industry, and promotes taste, traffic, and plenty. I sell the same trifles to neighboring nations at a much dearer rate than to you, and in that way I am useful to my country."

Babouc, after a moment's reflection, scratched the man's name out of his pocket book.

"For after all," said he, "the arts that minister to luxury multiply and flourish in a country only when all the necessary arts are also practiced, and the nation is numerous and wealthy. Ithuriel seems to me a little too severe."

Chapter 7

BABOUC, MUCH PUZZLED as to what opinion he ought to have of Persepolis, determined to visit the magi and men of letters, for, inasmuch as the former devote themselves to religion and the latter to wisdom, he had great hopes that they would obtain pardon for the rest of the people. So next morning he repaired to a college of the magi. The archimandrite acknowledged that he had an income of a hundred thousand crowns for having taken a vow of poverty, and that he exercised a very extensive dominion in virtue of his profession of humility; after which he left Babouc in the hands of a brother of low degree, who did the honors of the place.

While this brother was showing him all the magnificence of that home of penitence, a rumor spread that he was come to reform all those religious houses. He immediately began to receive memorials from each of them, all of which were substantially to this effect: "Preserve us, and destroy all the others."

To judge by the arguments that were used in self-defense, these societies were all absolutely necessary; if their mutual accusations were to be believed, they all alike deserved extinction. He marveled how there was not one of them but wished to govern the whole world in order to enlighten it. Then a little fellow, who was a demi-magian, came forward and said to him:

"I see clearly that the work is going to be accomplished, for Zerdust has returned to earth; little girls prophesy, getting themselves pinched in front and whipped behind. It is evident that the world is coming to an end; could you not, before the final catastrophe, protect us from the grand lama?"

"What nonsense!" said Babouc. "From the grand lama? From the pontiff-king who resides in Thibet?"

"Yes," said the little demi-magian, with a decided air; "against him, and none else."

"Then you wage war on him, and have armies?" asked Babouc.

"No," said the other, "but we have written three or four thousand books against him, that nobody reads, and as many pamphlets, which are read by women at our direction.[6] He has hardly ever heard us spoken of, he has only pronounced sentence against us, as a master might order the trees in his garden to be cleared of caterpillars."

Babouc shuddered at the folly of those men who made a profession of wisdom; the intrigues of those who had renounced the world; the ambition, greed, and pride of those who taught humility and unselfishness; and he came to the conclusion that Ithuriel had very good reason for destroying the whole brood.

Chapter 8

ON HIS RETURN to his lodging, he sent for some new books in order to soothe his indignation, and he invited some literary men to dinner for the sake of cheerful society. Twice as many came as he had asked, like wasps attracted by honey. These parasites were as eager to speak as they were to eat, and two classes of persons were the objects of their praise: the dead and their own selves,—never their contemporaries, the master of the house excepted. If one of them happened to make a clever remark, the countenances of all the others fell, and they gnawed their lips for vexation that it was not they who had said it. They did not disguise their real feelings so much as the magi, because their ambition was not pitched so high. There was not one of them but was soliciting some petty post or another, and at the same time wishing to be thought a great man. They said to each other's face the most insulting things, which they took for flashes of wit. Having some knowledge of Babouc's mission, one of them begged him in a whisper to annihilate an author who had not praised him as much as he thought proper, five years ago; another entreated the ruin of a citizen for having never laughed at his comedies; and a third desired the abolition of the Academy, because he himself had never succeeded in gaining admission. When the meal was finished, each went out by himself, for in all the company there were not two men who could endure or even speak a civil word to each other, outside the houses of those rich patrons who invited them to their table. Babouc deemed that it would be no great loss if all that breed of vermin were to perish in the general destruction.

Chapter 9

As SOON AS he was rid of them, he began to read some of the new books, and recognized in them the same temper as his guests had shown. He saw with special indignation those gazettes of slander, those records of bad taste which are dictated by envy, baseness, and abject poverty; those cowardly satires in which the vulture is treated with respect while the dove is torn to pieces; and those novels, destitute of imagination, in which are displayed so many portraits of women with whom the author is totally unacquainted.

He threw all those detestable writings into the fire, and went out to take an evening stroll. He was introduced to an old scholar who had not made one of his late company of parasites, for he always avoided the crowd. Knowing men well, he made good use of his knowledge, and was careful to whom he gave his confidence. Babouc spoke to him with indignation of what he had read and what he had seen.

"You have been reading poor contemptible stuff," said the learned sage; "but at all times, in all countries, and in every walk of life, the bad swarm and the good are rare. You have entertained the mere scum of pedantry, for in all professions alike those who least deserve to appear always obtrude themselves with most effrontery. The men of real wisdom live a quiet and retired life; there are still among us some men and books worthy of your attention."

While he was speaking thus another man of letters joined them, and their conversation was so agreeable and instructive, so superior to prejudice and conformable to virtue, that Babouc confessed he had never heard anything like it before.

"Here are men," he said to himself, "whom the angel Ithuriel will not dare to touch, or he will be ruthless indeed."

Reconciled as he now was to the men of letters, Babouc was still enraged at the rest of the nation.

"You are a stranger," said the judicious person who was talking to him; "abuses present themselves to your eyes in a mass, and the good which is concealed, and which sometimes springs out of these abuses, escapes your observation."

Then he learned that among the men of literature there were some who were free from envy, and that even among the magi virtuous men were to be found. He understood at last that these great societies, which seemed by their mutual collisions to be bringing about their common ruin, were in the main beneficial institutions; that each community of magi was a check upon its rivals; that if they differed in some matters of opinion, they all taught the same principles of morality, instructed the people, and lived in obedience to the laws, like tutors who watch over the son of the house, while the master watches over them. Becoming acquainted with several of these magi, he saw souls of heavenly disposition. He found that even among the simpletons who aspired to make war on the grand lama there had been some very great men. He began to suspect that the character of the people of Persepolis might be like their buildings, some of which had seemed to him deplorably bad, while others had ravished him with admiration.

Chapter 10

SAID BABOUC TO his literary friend:

"I see clearly enough that these magi, whom I thought so dangerous, are in reality very useful, especially when a wise government prevents them from making themselves too indispensable. But you will at least acknowledge that your young magistrates, who buy a seat on the bench as soon as they have learned to mount a horse, must needs display in your courts of law the most ridiculous incompetence and the most perverse injustice; it would undoubtedly be better to give these appointments gratuitously to those old lawyers who have passed all their lives in weighing conflicting arguments."

The man of letters made reply:

"You saw our army before your arrival at Persepolis; you know that our young officers fight very well, although they have purchased their commissions; perhaps you will find that our young magistrates do not pronounce wrong judgments, in spite of having paid for the positions they occupy."

He took Babouc the next day to the High Court of Judicature, where an important decision was to be delivered. The case was one that excited universal interest. All the old advocates who spoke about it were uncertain in their opinions. They quoted a hundred laws, not one of which had any essential bearing upon the question; they regarded the matter from a hundred points of view, none of which presented it in its true light. The judges were quicker in giving their decision than the advocates in raising doubts; their judgment was almost unanimous, and their sentence was just, because they followed the light of reason, whereas the others went astray in their opinions, because they had only consulted their books.

Babouc came to the conclusion that abuses often entail very good results. He had an opportunity of seeing that very day how the riches of the farmers of the revenue, which had given him so much offense, might produce an excellent effect, for the emperor, being in want of money, obtained in an hour by their means a sum that he would not have been able to procure in six months through the ordinary channels. He saw that those big clouds, swollen with the dews of earth, restored to it in rain all that they received from it. Moreover, the children of those self-made men, often better educated than those of the most ancient families, were sometimes of much greater value to their country; for there is nothing to hinder a man from making a good judge, a brave soldier, or a clever statesman, in the circumstance of his having had a good accountant for his father.

Chapter 11

By degrees Babouc forgave the greed of the farmers of the revenue, who are not in reality more greedy than other men, and who are necessary to the welfare of the state. He excused the folly of those who impoverished themselves in order to be a judge or a soldier, a folly which creates great magistrates and heroes. He pardoned the envy displayed by the men of letters, among whom were to be found men who enlightened the world; he became reconciled to the ambitious and intriguing magi, among whom eminent virtues outweighed petty vices. But there remained behind abundant matter of offense: above all, the love affairs of the ladies.

And the ruin which he felt sure must follow, filled him with disquietude and alarm.

As he wished to gain an insight into human life under all conditions, he procured an introduction to a minister of state, but on his way he was trembling all the time lest some wife should be assassinated by her husband before his eyes. On arriving at the statesman's house, he had to wait two hours in the antechamber before he was announced, and two hours more after that had been done. He fully made up his mind during that interval to report to the angel Ithuriel both the minister and his insolent lackeys. The antechamber was filled with ladies of every degree, with magi of all shades of opinion, with judges, tradesmen, officers, and pedants; all found fault with the minister. The misers and usurers said: "That fellow plunders the provinces, there's no doubt about it." The capricious reproached him with being eccentric. The libertines said: "He thinks of nothing but his pleasures." The factious flattered themselves that they should soon see him ruined by a cabal. The women hoped that they might ere long have a younger minister.

Babouc heard their remarks, and could not help saying:

"What a fortunate man this is! He has all his enemies in his antechamber; he crushes under his heel those who envy him; he sees those who detest him groveling at his feet."

At last he was admitted, and saw a little old man stooping under the weight of years and business, but still brisk and full of energy.

He was pleased with Babouc, who thought him a worthy man, and their conversation became interesting. The minister confessed that he was very unhappy; that he passed for rich, but was really poor; that he was believed to be all powerful, yet was being constantly thwarted, that almost all his favors had been conferred on the ungrateful; and that amid the continual labors of forty years he had scarcely had a moment's peace. Babouc was touched with compassion, and thought that if this man had committed faults and the angel Ithuriel wished to punish him, he had no need to destroy him: it would be enough to leave him where he was.

Chapter 12

WHILE THE MINISTER and he were talking together, the fair dame with whom Babouc had dined, hastily entered, and in her eyes and on her forehead were seen symptoms of vexation and anger. She burst out into reproaches against the statesman; she shed tears; she complained bitterly that her husband had been refused a post to which his birth allowed him to aspire, and to which his services and his wounds entitled him. She expressed herself so forcibly, she made her complaints with so much grace, she overcame objections with such skill and reinforced her arguments with such eloquence, that ere she left the room she had made her husband's fortune.

Babouc held out his hand, and said:

"Is it possible, madam, that you can have given yourself all this trouble for a man whom you do not love, and from whom you have everything to fear?"

"A man whom I do not love!" she cried. "My husband, let me tell you, is the best friend I have in the world; there is nothing that I would not sacrifice for him, except my lover, and he would do anything for me, except giving up his mistress. I should like you to know her; she is a charming woman, full of wit, and of an excellent disposition; we sup together this evening with my husband and my little magian; come and share our enjoyment."

The lady took Babouc home with her. The husband, who had arrived at last, overwhelmed with grief, saw his wife again with transports of delight and gratitude; he embraced by turns his wife, his mistress, the little magian, and Babouc. Unity, cheerfulness, wit, and elegance were the soul of the repast.

"Learn," said the fair dame at whose house he was supping, "that those who are sometimes called women of no virtue have almost always merits as genuine as those of the most honorable man; and to convince yourself of it come with me tomorrow and dine with the fair Theona. There are some old vestals who pick her to pieces, but she does more good than all of them together. She would not commit even a trifling act of injustice to promote her own interests, however important; the advice she gives her lover is always noble; his glory is her sole concern; he would blush to face her if he had neglected any occasion of doing good; for a man can have no greater encouragement to virtuous actions than to have for a witness and judge of his conduct a mistress whose good opinion he is anxious to deserve."

Babouc did not fail to keep the appointment. He saw a house where all the pleasures reigned, with Theona at their head, who knew how to speak in the language of each. Her natural good sense put others at their ease; she made herself agreeable without an effort, for she was as amiable as she was generous, and, what enhanced the value of all her good qualities, she was beautiful.

Babouc, Scythian though he was, and though a spirit had sent him on his mission, perceived that, if he stayed any longer at Persepolis, he should forget Ithuriel for Theona. He felt fond of a city whose inhabitants were polite, good-humored and kind, however frivolous they might be, greedy of scandal, and full of vanity. He feared that the doom of Persepolis was sealed; he dreaded, too, the report he would have to give.

This was the method he adopted for making that report. He gave instructions to the best founder in the city to cast a small image composed of all kinds of metals, earth, and stones, alike the most precious and the most worthless. He brought it to Ithuriel, and said:

"Wilt thou break this pretty little image because it is not all gold and diamonds?"

Ithuriel understood his meaning before the words were out of his mouth, and determined that he would not think of punishing Persepolis, but would let the world go on in its own way; "for," said he, "if everything is not as it should be, there is nothing intolerably bad." So Persepolis was allowed to remain unharmed, and Babouc was very far from uttering any complaint like Jonah, who was angry because Nineveh was not destroyed. But when a man has been three days in a whale's belly, he is not so good-tempered as after a visit to the opera or to the play, or after having supped in good company.

Endnotes

Zadig, or Destiny (pages 1–68)

1. Reference is to a popular form of quack medicine practiced in Voltaire's time.
2. The name Yebor is an anagram of the last name of Jean-Francois Boyer, a French bishop and philosophical antagonist of Voltaire.
3. The reference is to another contemporary antagonist of Voltaire, the Abbé Pierre Desfontaines (1685–1745).
4. Reference here is the philosophical system of Leibniz.
5. Reference is to an eighteenth-century book on Eastern philosophy.
6. That poisonous serpents stung with their tongues was a common popular misconception in Voltaire's time.
7. Li and Tien refer to Chinese words meaning reason and heaven.
8. Serendib was a name for Ceylon in the Arabian Nights.
9. The Greek word refers to exceptionally beautiful women. The word *bonzes* in this section refers to Japanese or Chinese Buddhist monks.
10. The story recounted in this section has its origin in the medieval collection, Gesta Romanorum.

Micromégas (pages 69–86)

1. The name "Micromégas" may be read to mean "small/large" or "the little great one…"
2. The reference is to William Derham (1657–1735) author of Astro-Theology: Or, a Demonstration of the Being and Attributes of God From a Survey of the Heavens (1731).
3. The reference is to Christiaan Huyghens (1629–1695), discoverer of the rings of Saturn and the first of Saturn's moons, Titan.

4. Louis Moréri's (1643–1680) *Grand Dictionnaire Historique et Critique* was first published in 1674.
5. Reference is to the work of Antonie van Leeuwenhoek (1632–1723) and Nicolaus Hartsaeker (1656–1725).
6. Reference is to a well-known remark by Bernard de Fontenelle (1657–1757).
7. Author of *Gulliver's Travels*, Jonathan Swift (1667–1745).
8. Type of headgear worn by Doctors from the Sorbonne in Paris in Voltaire's time.

Jeannot and Colin (pages 87–95)

1. Reference is to the work of Bernard de Fontenelle (1657–1757).
2. The reference is to Louis II (846–879), known as the Stammerer, a son of Charles the Bald.
3. The Theatines were a religious order.

The World Is Like That, or the Vision of Babouc (pages 105–120)

1. Reference is to the wars between England and France.
2. A coin of modest value.
3. The reference is to a quarter of Paris formerly known as Saint Marceau.
4. The ancient Pictavians were inhabitants of the province of Poitou in west central France.
5. The Hotel des Invalides in Paris.
6. Reference is to the Jansenist theological controversies of Voltaire's time.